ROGER

LADIES LOVE TO PAY HIM

RICHARD LEE

RICHARD LEE PUBLISHING

*Dedicated to a world in need of
love and imagination.*

"You only live once, but if you do it right, once is enough." Mae West

FOREWORD

The young Roger Robertson has left university and is planning a career in law.

At a post-university one-day advanced sex education seminar, Roger meets a sex worker who enriches his life choices for ever.

PREFACE

A soft but firm sensuous voice then addressed the class and every young man was immediately smitten.

"Girls have wet dreams, too!"

Mary gave us all a few moments to digest what she had just said and my mind was immediately thrown into turmoil. How was it that I didn't already know this? How had this been kept a secret from me for so long? But then Mary was talking again.

"Women enjoy mens attention most when it is slow; when his persuasive manoeuvres lead the two to a gentle coming together to enjoy all of it's touching and kissing and sweet words.

"Men usually want things to happen faster; to get to the end point; to arrive at the moment of ejaculation.

"If they are lucky, men might learn the benefits of slowing down as they age which is unfortunate for both them and the young women they pursue."

ONE

SEX EDUCATION

Our final year university student activities included sexual education classes. I doubted whether they would be very informative, and I also thought it wouldn't help me with my problem; being attracted to much older women. But I agreed to join my mates and check it out.

The first class was relatively simple and included male and female students.

When we turned up for our first 'men only' class, things changed considerably, and it wasn't long before all the lads were immersed in an experience we'd each remember for the rest of our lives.

We dutifully wore our name tags, having been told it was essential for this part of the component.

Howard Humphries, the coordinator, stood before his chosen dozen. Beside him was a substantially built, attractive older woman. I estimated her to be in her early to mid-fifties. She had a lovely smile, and her dark eyes shone, suggesting enthusiasm for the subject we were there to learn about. She wore tight clothing, which accentuated her full figure most pleasantly.

"This delightful lady is Mary, and she is a member of an association which provides counselling services and practical hands-on instruction for sex therapists and educational organisations like ours. Mary is also a registered sex worker."

Mary's smile broadened, and she waved to everyone.

"This evening, we will go quite a bit further with our exploration of the subject of sex.

"With Mary's generous help, you will leave here having had an experience that you might have fantasied about but probably never had an opportunity to put into practice.

"And when I use the word fantasied, I should warn all of you that Mary is offering hands-on touching and feeling of her beautiful, full-bodied self. If anyone present feels that this is not something they should be a part of, then now is when you should leave the class. Leaving will not result in any loss of marks or access to future classes."

There was silence as Mr Humphries looked around the class. Mary maintained her mesmerising smile. No one rose and left.

"Okay then. Moving right along, Mary will now take over the class. She will begin by removing some of her clothing, and I should mention that if you are excited by what you see, please be respectful. No calling out or comments, thank you.

"I'll finish by saying, with a smile on my face, that all will be revealed just so long as you are patient. Thank you, Mary. The class is yours."

A soft but firm sensuous voice then addressed the class, and every man was immediately smitten.

"Girls have wet dreams, too!"

Mary gave us all a few moments to digest what she had just said, and it immediately threw me into turmoil. How was it that I didn't already know this? How had this been kept a secret from me for so long? But then Mary was talking again.

"There are similarities and differences between men and women, and while the tensions between the two sexes can bring them together, differences can sometimes keep them apart.

"So I will deal with the problematic side of things first.

"Women enjoy men's attention most when it is slow; when his persuasive manoeuvres lead the two to a gentle coming together to enjoy all of its touching and kissing and sweet words.

"Men usually want things to happen faster, to get to the endpoint, to arrive at the moment of ejaculation.

"Men only learn the benefits of slowing down as they age, which is unfortunate for both them and the young women they pursue."

The students around me sat in stunned silence. I could feel them all holding their breath. This person was talking about them as no one had spoken before, and every one of them could feel it.

Then came the bombshell. Mary unbuttoned her blouse and slowly removed it, displaying her pale skin and a lacy bra. Then she walked around to the front of the table, turned her back towards us, unzipped her skirt, and let it drop to the floor.

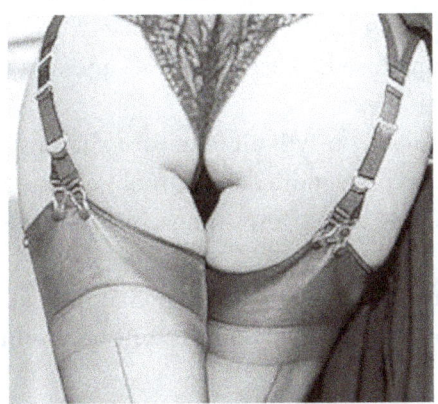

There was a soft buzz around me as classmates gasped and let go of their tensions. They moved their legs and arms and shuffled their feet as though they were preparing for the next event.

Eyes fed on the apparition in front of them. They had seen this sort of thing on porn websites, but this voluptuous woman in heels and stockings and garter belt and lacy knickers and bra, smiling at them and talking to them was the real thing. And every young man believed that Mary had eyes only for them.

"Do you like seeing me like this, lads? Are you getting horny? We girls don't know what effect we have on you until you react.

"So let me see a show of hands if you are turned on by how I look?"

Every arm reached up, including Mr Humphries, and Mary beamed a happy smile to everyone.

"Well, thank you all. And thank you, Howard. I appreciate it."

Mary looked across at the now red-faced man. Then her head tilted as she scanned the lower part of his body. Then she turned and smiled knowingly at us.

She faced the audience and put a hand beside her mouth to shield it, pretending she didn't want Mr Howard to hear and whispered, "I can see that he means it."

A couple of us chuckled.

"Perhaps you could come and stand a little closer, Howard. I'll need you to help out shortly. And it's reassuring to know that you will be a willing helper to a lady needing a man's attention."

Mr Humphries moved to stand beside Mary, making sure his hands were folded and hiding the front of his trousers.

Mary moved up close to Mr Humphries and slid an arm around his waist.

"In a few minutes, you will all take turns having a private moment with me. You may have noticed the mobile changing room set up behind me. There are a just few things in life that should be experienced in private.

"You will be invited, one at a time, to visit me in the changing room before exiting and leaving the room. It will be the final activity of the afternoon.

"Don't be alarmed. I'm about to demonstrate what you will experience.

"Howard, darling, will you kindly push your hand down inside the back of my knickers and fondle my buttocks, please?

"Fondling, caressing and touching with your fingertips will get you a long way with your girlfriends. Just remember to do everything slowly. Oh, yes! And never underestimate the power of kissing."

The red-faced Howard now seemed oblivious to his students, and we watched as he did what he was told.

When his hand was well inside Mary's knickers, she turned and smiled at us, but not before she unbuckled Howard's belt and slid her hand down inside Howard's trousers.

Mary grasped, and Howard gasped, and we could all see her hand moving backwards and forwards, or was it up and down? Then the woman with the wicked smile turned enough so that we could all see her backside, pushing it out and shaking it provocatively to a very appreciative audience.

Mary seemed not to want to let go of Howard's cock still hidden in his trousers.

But then Mary straightened herself up and gently took Howard's hand in hers.

"Thank you all. You've been a most attentive audience. I will now move into the changing room, where I look forward to meeting you in person.

"Howard? Would you send the young men in one at a time, please? I will ring a bell when I'm ready for the next visitor.

"Oh, yes. And Howard? Please don't run off when they're all finished. I will want a word if you know what I mean. I'll need you to complete my wet dream, darling."

A bell rang, and Mr Humphries called my name and pointed to the tent entrance. I was the third person to enter the tent and meet Mary.

As I moved the curtain aside and entered, the magnificent Mary took my hand and leant me against the edge of a mobile massage table positioned along one side of the tiny room.

Her bra had gone, as had her knickers. She wore only her garter belt and stockings and shoes. Her eyes shone, and she ran her tongue over her bright red lips in what looked like anticipation. She took my hand and moved it down to her mesmerising hairy crotch.

"Now, Roger, feel my pussy, please."

She placed her big lipsticked lips against mine while both her hands unzipped my trousers.

Mary quickly found and liberated my cock, and moments later, she had squatted down and popped it into her mouth, making loud sucking and slurping sounds. Playing with my testicles with one hand, Mary's other hand pushed my fingers up into her very wet vulva, moving them around quite vigorously. Just moments later, the huge woman's body shook.

Suddenly it was all over, and Mary was tucking me back into my trousers. Then she looked into my eyes and laughed, whispering a final message.

"Sorry, we don't have time, Roger. But can you keep a secret?"

I nodded that I could.

"You have a wonderful cock which I would love to meet up with again soon when we could have more time together.

"If you would like to see me so that we can enjoy each other properly, come to the Charity Shop in Spring Street just before we lock up at 5 pm on any Monday. It must be on a Monday.

"If another shop assistant offers to help, say you're looking for shirts. That will ensure that they call me. Everyone leaves about then, and I am left to lock up. We would be alone together. Please say you will come, Roger?"

In my confusion, I murmured that I would and managed a smile.

"Oh, thank you, Roger. Helping a woman make her wet dreams come true is such a worthwhile cause. I'll make sure you are fully rewarded, I promise."

Mary kissed me lovingly and rubbed my hand on her substantial stiff nipples, and as she shuddered again, she whispered, "Oh, yes, Roger. Don't forget me, you darling man."

I was suddenly out of the tent and in the corridor and stumbling along, trying to collect my thoughts and body together. Then I heard a bell ring behind me. Student number four was about to help dear Mary fulfil her dreams.

If Mary's wet-dream world lived in the present, I couldn't help but wonder what she dreamt about at night? But then I knew what I would be dreaming about tonight.

TWO

SHOPPING FOR SHIRTS

A few people were leaving the Charity Shop as I approached. Why was I feeling so self-conscious? What if I met someone I knew? Fellow students, especially female students, used the shop regularly.

"Hello, Roger! I think you might be too late. They're about to close. Kaz and I are going for a coffee at the cafe down the road. You are welcome to join us if you want to."

I froze up inside. This was the lovely Lucy who I had long wanted to ask out and couldn't pluck up the courage to do so.

Lucy was the one woman around my age that I was attracted to. Lucy was doing medical science while I was studying law. There was just something about her. And now, here she was offering me the opportunity I'd longed for. Maybe there was a god! Have they sent Lucy to save me from a life of debauchery?

My mind was in turmoil. Every possible vaguely connected snippet ran past me. 'A bird in the hand is worth two in the bush', and, 'if it seems too good to be true, then it probably isn't true.' And what was my mother's voice doing here? "Just don't come home pushing a pram, son," and "keep yourself nice if you want to get the best out of life."

Lust saved me! What lived between my legs overrode the subtle emotions of the heart. I smiled lovingly at Lucy and thanked her, then I lied!

"I'm just picking up some shirts I put aside. Then I have a late appointment at my dad's friend's chambers about possible work in the holidays. I'd love to catch up sometime, though."

I immediately turned away and didn't bother to look at her face to see her reaction. Other things urged me on.

Inside the shop, a woman was saying goodbye to the last customer. She held a door key in her hand. She turned and looked at me. Her face softened, and she smiled. I thought she would tell me that the shop was about to close, but she didn't. Instead, she walked from behind the counter and stood in front of me, smiling and announced that her name was Julie.

I nearly blurted out that I was here to see Mary but managed not to.

"Hello, Julie. I'm Roger."

I estimated that Julie was around the same age as Mary. She had that same haunting look that spoke of things that young men searched for, except they didn't know precisely what those things were they were looking for.

If I had known what I know now, I would have said that Julie looked hot even if she wasn't dressed provocatively. So much for hindsight.

Her hair was tied back in a bun, and a pale cardigan covered the top of her relatively short floral dress. Julie could have passed for anyone's mum or the neighbour's wife. It was her legs and feet that begged for attention. Shapely legs with light stockings and medium heeled shoes completed a picture of clear promise. But it was her face that did it for me. How do men resist the look a woman can wear at certain times and convince a man that he is the only male she could ever be interested in.

"How can I help you, Roger?" Julie spoke with the strange prescient confidence of prior knowledge.

"I was looking for shirts, Julie."

Then came the shock announcement.

"Mary, who looks after men's clothing, called in sick this morning, so maybe I can help?"

The beautiful housewife – come, auntie – come, motherly matron – come best friends sister-in-law – come, every other older woman that understood the real world – beamed at me, and I couldn't think of a thing to say.

Julie asked me to wait for just a moment while she locked the front door.

"You're the lucky last. Maybe I can help. Follow me, Roger."

I was perplexed. Was I going to leave shortly with an arm full of shirts?

Halfway along an aisle of coats and jumpers, Julie stopped and turned and smiled.

"As Mary couldn't be here, she mentioned the possibility of you calling in, and she asked would I mind passing on a kiss from her. Is that okay, Roger? You're such a handsome young man. Mary gets all the attention, and I do get a little bit envious of her. We would fulfil her request, and I could enjoy a little excitement as well. You would be doing a lonely lady a great favour.

Julie moved up closer. Her eyes appealed like almond blossom to a bee. She put out her arms, and I stepped into them, and moments later, I melted into her, and we were kissing and moving our arms around as we rubbed each other's shoulders and squeezed each other's waists. Then she put a hand on the front of my trousers and gasped as she discovered my rising level of interest.

Julie pulled away and stared at me. Then she took me by the hand and led me to the end of the aisle and a door leading into a restroom of some sort, complete with a bed for staff or customers that might take sick.

Julie turned and looked at me.

"Will I take off my clothes, Roger, or would you like to do it?"

For the first time in my life, my manhood stood up to be counted. "I'll do it, Julie," I muttered.

She smiled and closed her eyes and whispered back to me, "Take your time darling, I love being stripped. Just love it!"

I started with the cardigan. That was uneventful apart from the symbolism of its removal, indicating Julie's willingness to be the centre of my sexual attention.

Julie giggled when I had trouble with the zip on the back of her dress, and she was forced to come to my aid. Then she shimmied, and the garment fell to the floor. The newly discovered Galant in me took her by the hand, and she stepped out of her dress and stood in her matching purple bra and pants and garter belt and tan stockings and low heels.

I stared at her, and again, the new me was moved to speak and act.

"You are lovely, Julie. I want to kiss and touch you all over. May I?"

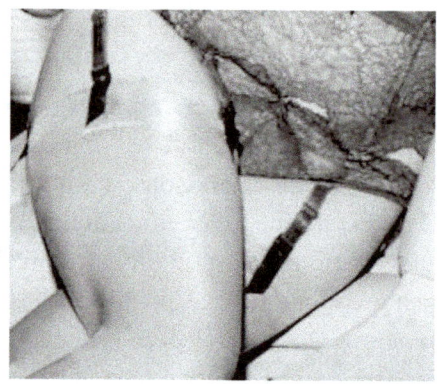

Whether it was my gentlemanly manner or just the heat of the moment, she replied in a tiny, almost pleading voice.

"Oh, yes, Roger, do whatever you want with me. I'm yours. Oh, and Roger? Would you please ask me to do anything? And can I take your cock out? It looks as though it would like to join the party."

I laughed in appreciation of this delightful woman's free and easy manner.

"Please do that, Julie, before it rips a hole in my pants."

As the dear lady took me from my dungeon, I slid a hand down into her bra and discovered a shapely and welcoming breast and a stiff nipple, all of which fed into my now completely enthralled sensual world. And when Julie popped my stiff cock into her mouth and began to enjoy herself, I slipped off her bra and took hold of two beautiful breasts and fingered two perky nipples.

"Now lay back on the bed Julie and let me take off the rest of your clothes."

The dear woman let out a tiny moan and took my member from her mouth and, without letting go of it, sat back with her legs perched over the edge of the bed.

I stared down in appreciation, knowing she was watching me through half-open eyes.

I wanted to eat all of her at once. I put my hands on her thighs, not sure whether to move them up or down. As if to encourage me in a particular direction, she lifted herself and stretched out her legs and moaned again, and my hands moved up. I took hold of her tiny pants and dragged them down, stopping part-way to look at her tuft of blond hair and notice the wet smear beside it on her thigh. Then I pulled her knickers down and off and tossed them away.

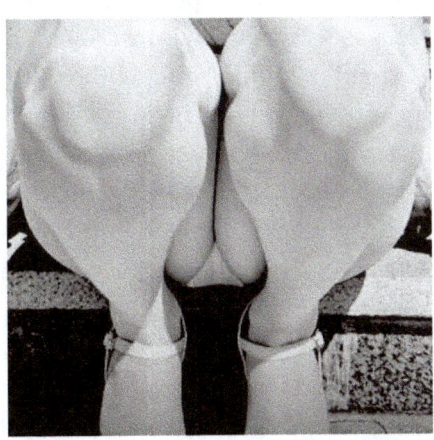

Julie's hand tightened its hold on my cock, and she pulled at it and stared up at me, indicating that she wanted it in her mouth again.

I lifted her legs and laid her out on the bed. Then I lifted my leg over the top of her body. While Julie gasped and moaned and fed me back into her mouth, I stared close-up at my first vulva. The perfume was exquisite, and I cautiously moved my index finger onto the soft pink wet part nestling in her pubic hair.

"Oh yes, Roger. Yes, touch me, my darling. Finger my pussy. Explore my wet cunt. It's yours. Do anything, Roger."

I was in heaven, and my mouth soon found its way to her magic place. Her stockinged thighs and suspenders rubbed my cheeks and called out to be groped and kissed and fondled, and that is what I did until suddenly, Julie screamed and threw herself up and came against my chin and my nose, then collapsed back down, pushing my wet face back in between her legs.

"Oh, God. You are wonderful, Roger. Just don't stop. Please, please, don't stop!"

Julie orgasmed again and then again, then the beautiful woman pulled my head away as she lay panting and moaning.

"Oh, Roger, it's your turn now, dear man. Turn around and fuck me. And come inside me. I desperately want that."

My first woman was asking me to do it to her. I quickly turned my body around. As I did, so she grabbed my head and covered my face with kisses, licking and enjoying the perfume of her cunt on my lips.

"Oh, my God! This is so wonderful. Just keep doing whatever you want to do to me, Roger. I'm loving being with you."

A moment later, Julie took hold of my very stiff appendage and guided it into her wet vagina, and I was in heaven. I just lay there, not wanting to move. Just the feel of her soft, warm, damp pussy clasping my cock was beyond my wildest dreams. But then she trembled, and she began to move ever so slightly, backwards and forwards, and I responded ever so slowly, moving in and out, gaining momentum and testing the boundaries of this beautiful new place.

There was no point in delaying my ejaculation, and I came forcibly, my cock pushing hard against her pelvic bone. Julie screamed and spoke gibberish and shook violently.

I withdrew and stared down at my first loving partner. Julie looked beautiful. A serene smile through half-open eyes greeted me.

"Did I make you a happy young man? You did it for me, Roger, my dear. Please accept my heartfelt thanks."

I looked down at the womanly form beneath me. Why couldn't I keep fucking her forever? Then all of a sudden, my cock twitched.

"I haven't finished with you yet, Julie. Open your legs again and put me in."

Julie's eyes opened wide, and her mouth fell open as she scrambled to do what I asked. Then I surrendered totally to my desires, thrusting like a madman for maybe a minute before I came with a roar that I didn't recognise as my voice.

Julie lay crying, and I cradled her in my arms, crushing her breasts against my chest. We lay like that for quite some time. Then I felt her hand on the side of my head as she sought out my face and lips. We kissed, and I discovered a new heaven.

THREE
STEP MUM AND STEP SISTER

My recent experience with the fantastic Julie had rapidly brought me to a new sense of myself, and I was excited about what life could be like.

Young women excited me but not as much as older women. Every attractive older woman that crossed my path set my imagination on fire, and it was all I could do to stop myself from moving towards them and opening up a conversation.

My mother had died when I was only seven, and my father, Andy, had remarried when I was 16.

Amelia was a much younger woman. She was a lawyer, and they had met through work. Amelia and I got on very well. Even though she was twenty-five years older than me, it was in some ways like having a big sister. She had never had to discipline me like I was a child, and I never had to express anger or frustration at being restrained.

We all got on very well, and my father enjoyed and partook in our foolish banter, though less so when it came to movies or television soaps.

Amelia's younger sister, Emily, would sometimes visit. She lived in a studio apartment close to the university but would often visit for a meal or go with us to the beach at weekends. Dad was a keen surfer, as was I, and so we enjoyed great times together.

We all loved our regular visits to the beach, which wasn't far from where we lived.

Amelia and her sister would enjoy teasing me, especially when a couple of bikini-clad young women passed by.

They loved it that they could observe my embarrassment and laughed loudly.

As I grew older and more confident, I would chase the two teasing women around on the sand or into the water, threatening to drag down their bathers and expose their bodies. They still regarded me as a big kid and harmless, even though I had turned 20.

Occasionally, when there wasn't a boyfriend in tow, Emily would take things a bit further.

She and her older sister, dressed in their bikinis, would sneak up and jump on me when I was sunbathing.

Amelia would sit on me and hold me down, and Emily would drag down my bathers and smack my bare backside hard with her sandal, not stopping until Amelia intervened.

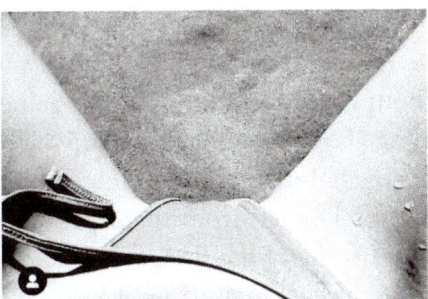

"You'd better stop, sis, or he might end up as kinky as you. And fix your bloody bikini. You're such a slut."

My ego was hurt as much as my backside, and when I eventually broke free, I would pull up my pants and disappear, hiding my teary red face and massaging my rear.

Occasionally I would overhear the sisters talking about Emily's fraught love-life, which I wasn't interested in. I purposely avoided interrupting their women's business at those moments.

I would hear them laugh loudly occasionally, and I couldn't help wondering what they were discussing. And I regularly listened to my stepmother utter the words, "It's always the same, Emily. For goodness sake, try someone different. Stop going out with almost identical older men where it's simply too late for them to change. Get a man you can train."

Then Emily would fight back. "So that is what you did, dear sister?"

Then I heard Amelia's angry voice.

"I found the perfect man who had already had a very aware and perfect wife who trained him well. And most importantly, from the very outset, we talked about everything, including what we wanted. I was fortunate. So there!"

Emily would regularly bring a boyfriend to the beach. It was a different man every time, and I was usually the beneficiary of that man's nervous attention as he tried to glean helpful information about my aunt.

By the time we had walked along the beach and back, each man would return without any special knowledge gained from me. I just didn't know anything about my aunt or her private life.

However, what was helpful about my interactions with all of these men was the amount I learned from them about women. Not that I wasn't sceptical about some of the things they told me, but over time, patterns emerged so that eventually, I felt I knew quite a bit about the fair sex. Indeed, I discovered much more about my aunt Emily's interactions with her men.

These talking and walking beach affairs followed a predictable pattern. "What will you do when you leave university?" "Which football team did I barrack for?" "What is your favourite hobby?" and so on. But slowly, the men's voices would change as they each began to talk about relationships and, in particular, their relationship with my aunt.

They would suddenly appear overcome by a haunting sadness or despair. Their voices would change, and some even showed emotion.

"She gets so emotional." "She's got such a short fuse." "She won't say why she doesn't like to be touched in that spot." "She claims I'm as sensitive as a house brick." "She doesn't like my underpants." "She says she hates dresses and skirts." "She says I'm too rough." "She thinks I'm not manly enough."

The list went on and on, and sometimes I just gave up listening. After a year or so, I began to think poorly of Emily, but eventually, those negative thoughts morphed into my feeling a bit sorry for her.

———————

"Roger?"

"Yes, Amelia?"

"I just called Emily to tell her that I'd finished the alterations to the dress she bought. She said she couldn't get over here as she had a lot on. She asked if I could ask you if you would be going into the university tomorrow, and if you were, could you drop the dress into her."

"Sure! Happy to do that. Tell her I'll come by at around 5.30 after I've finished in the library."

"Okay! Thanks. Oh, and you might need to wait a little while so that she can try the dress on and in case I need to make more alterations."

"I thought she didn't like wearing dresses?"

Amelia stopped what she was doing and looked across the room at me. Her face looked most serious.

"What makes you say that, Roger?"

"Oh, I don't know. Probably one of her boyfriends at the beach one year mentioned it. Can't remember."

Amelia continued to stare at me.

"Did you talk to many of her boyfriends, Roger?"

"All of them. The walking wounded, I called them. Nice bunch of blokes, mostly, but a bit sad. I assumed that's what happens when you get to their age, and you still hadn't discovered the meaning of life."

Amelia's mouth opened, and she wore a look of disbelief.

"And you have discovered the meaning of life, have you, Roger?" She spoke quietly.

"Well, not all of it, Amelia. Just the boy girl-part of it."

"And that is?"

I looked at my step mums face and smiled.

"Never have just one girlfriend. At least not until you are sure you've found the right one. People expect too much of each other."

"So would you fall in love and settle down, Roger?"

"Eventually, I suppose. I expect I'll find someone who I like and who I could be friends with. It might work out. You and dad seem good."

Amelia was trying to process what I had said, and her face changed every few seconds each time she thought of something she wanted to ask me.

"So, Roger? How many girlfriends do you have now?"

I laughed and wondered what she was thinking and what my response should be. I didn't want her to worry about me.

"Well, Amelia, I'm not sure if we need to talk about my love life. Perhaps if I just tell you that I'm currently well provided for by a couple of older women and I'm pleased with my lot. Would that be enough?"

Amelia's face suddenly looked shocked.

"It indeed would not, young man. What on earth do you mean, two older women? A couple of randy Cougars have caught you? Do they give you money?

"I will have a chat with your dad. He will love to hear about you being well provided for. He did once mention that he wondered when you would start bringing girls home.

"I might not mention the older women part, at least not until I've wheedled more information out of you. He might just want to meet them. And it might be dangerous.

"A father, son and Cougar foursome? Oh my God, it doesn't bear thinking about."

Despite my stepmother's genuine concern, we both enjoyed our banter.

"Don't think this conversation is over, young man."

"Now, there is one last thing you need to know. You won't be talking to Emily's boyfriends at the beach anymore."

"Oh, Christ! Has she run out of men?"

"No, it's just that her new partner is a woman. Andrea wants Emily to wear a dress at a big celebration coming up at the gay club they visit.

"Now, this is all supposed to be a secret, so you know nothing about it. Please, please, don't let Emily know that you know. Not a hint. Okay?"

I couldn't believe what I was hearing.

"Sure thing! No gay talk, I promise."

I was friends with a couple of lesbians at college, and I liked their down to earth manner. And then there was always talk about some of the female students having special girly moments together, and bisexual activity among the more arty ones was not uncommon, including among the men.

I stared back at Amelia.

"Well, I must say that this surprises me. But now I understand why all the walking wounded who talked to me on the beach failed so miserably. They just didn't have what she wanted. They could never have made her happy.

"I wish she'd found out earlier, though, for everybody's sake, including hers.

"Have you met Andrea, Amelia?"

"No, not yet. It's all very new, so my sister is taking things very slowly. She'll introduce her when she feels she's up to it.

FOUR

HAPPY REVENGE

Emily let me in and ushered me through to the kitchen. I passed her the bag with the dress and said that Amelia had suggested I wait while she tries it on.

Emily stopped moving about and listened. Then she visibly slumped as though the stresses of her life had momentarily disappeared.

"Thanks, Rog, that's a good idea. It might take a little while. Make yourself comfortable. The TV is in the lounge. Well, you already know that. Umm! There is food and drink in the fridge. Help yourself."

I looked at Emily and smiled my best friendly smile. If I carried misgivings about her because of all the talk with her ex-boyfriends, these now fell away. I suspected this was because of the latest information that Amelia had provided.

Whether it was my smile or just that moment in the day when you want to chill out, Emily was suddenly smiling back at me in a surprisingly friendly fashion.

She wore a high neck blue woollen sweater with black track pants and no shoes. Her shoulder-length dark hair hung loose. I had never seen her wear make-up, but she did have lipstick on, and there was a hint of eye-shadow, and her toes were painted red.

"You seem to grow bigger every time I see you, Roger. Maybe you work out? Is life good for you at 24?"

I replied that I visited the gym once or twice a week, and yes, life was good, thank you.

I began to get the feeling that she wanted to talk but wasn't sure where to start. We had never really talked in the past, probably because she always saw me as just a big adolescent kid. Now it appeared that that might have changed.

"Do you have memories of our past holiday's, Roger?"

I assured Emily that I did.

"Why do you ask, Em?"

Emily lifted her legs onto the sofa and sat back on them, and looked at me as if for the first time. It was then that a thought crossed my mind. It was possible that recent events in her life and the new relationship with Andrea were causing her to reflect on her recent years. I couldn't be sure, but Emily seemed to be looking for something, looking for a way to approach her dramatically changed present situation by understanding her past.

"Did you like me when you were a teenager, Roger?"

I suddenly realised that this was an opportunity to clear the air for both of us, even if I needed to lie just a little.

"No, Emily, I thought you were a real bitch. But as I got older, I changed and began to think about you differently.

"Differently? In what way, Roger?"

"I began to see you as being a more sensual woman but hidden behind a mask of some sort. A couple of years back, I went through a stage of fantasising about you sexually. But it was different to what I might fantasise about other girls or women."

I heard Emily gasp, and I looked up and saw that her jaw had dropped and she was staring strangely at me. It was a look I'd seen on her face years ago, and I tried to place it but couldn't.

Emily's voice came slow and low, almost husky.

"Tell me more, Roger. How was I different? And Roger? Is your fantasy still there? I need to know?"

Emily looked at me with a strange passion in her eyes.

I realised that what happened here today could influence my aunt's situation, and if I was right, she needed to know the truth.

"I am obsessed with your beautiful backside, Emily. My fantasy revolves around me tearing off your pants and spanking you until you beg for more, or you beg for mercy.

"You made me cry when you beat me all those years ago, and now I want to take my revenge.

"I want your arse, and then I might even fuck it while I've got hold of it. Do you understand? You set this kinky seed with your own hands on those beach holidays. Now you can reap the benefit. You wouldn't regret it, Em, I promise you that.

Emily's face had changed. There appeared a kind of serenity that I had never seen on her face before. She looked as though she'd found something she thought was lost forever. Emily stared at me, and her eyes shone with a magic light.

A silence that words could not break lasted for what seemed forever. Then Emily rose and stood in front of me. She turned her back on me and took three steps over to the bed. With both hands, she dragged her sweater over her head and threw it across the room. Then she paused before pushing her yoga pants down to just below her buttocks, displaying her most beautiful and perfect bum.

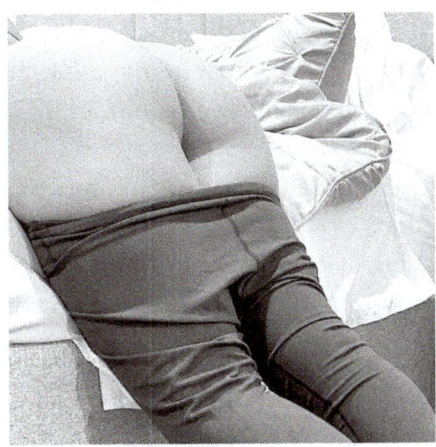

Then she leant forward and laid the top of her body on the bed, letting her shapely legs stretch out behind her. Her final move was thrusting her backside upwards and towards me. Then she turned her head and looked back at me and smiled and blew me a kiss.

"You're right, Roger. I'm a fucking slut, and I deserve all that you want to do to me. I'm yours, Roger. Come and take my arse. Punish me! Do everything you ever fantasised about doing to me. Everything!"

The look on Emily's face as she watched me slide my leather belt out of my trousers was one of both horror and then anticipation. Emily began muttering and moaning and her eyes widened as she watched as I stepped out of my clothes and pointed my now significantly enlarged cock in her direction.

I stepped over to the prone figure and removed her yoga pants, hearing her mumble excitedly.

"Yes!, oh yes! Yes, yes, yes, yes! Oh yes!"

I can't or won't attempt to describe everything that happened over the next two hours with Emily. Sufficient to say that the experience was momentous.

Emily did have a kink. I remembered that her sister had mentioned it in passing on one of our beach holidays many years ago. "You'd better stop, sis, or he might end up as kinky as you."

Emily had pulled down my swimming trunks and was thrashing my backside. A good memory accompanies an impressionable young mind.

At last, we were facing off, kink to kink. But spanking was not on my immediate agenda.

I don't know why I did the things that I did except that they happened naturally or unnaturally, depending on your point of view.

Beginning with dragging two sets of hard fingernails from her neck to her arse made her convulse and scream, and then I did it again.

Emily's screaming descended into heartfelt crying and sobbing. And when I rolled her over onto her back and repeated the nail dragging from her neck to her pubis, she screamed again and threw herself about. Her violent movement and utterances ended in her calling out, "Oh yes! Oh yes! Yes!"

I eventually found her endless loud crying and sobbing disconcerting, but when I took a moment out and asked her if she was okay, she snarled back. "Fine! Happy! Don't fucking ask me again. Just don't stop!"

I couldn't have expected a more solid indication of approval.

Without a second thought, I rolled her back over onto her stomach and pushed open her legs and fucked her very wet cunt as though it were just another piece of gym equipment; a workout to work up a healthy sweat.

I now had to accept that the more noise Emily made, the more it indicated she was getting what she wanted. In the midst of all of this frenzied expressions of lust, Emily suddenly arched her back and was at first silent before screaming to announce her orgasm. She threw herself around every which way, and then she reached down between her legs and grabbed my testicles to make sure my cock could not pull out.

When she had settled down a bit and without removing myself from her wet vagina, I repeated my nail torture, running my fingers from her ankle to her beautiful right buttock. Before I could get to her other leg, Emily arched her back again and screamed.

"You fucking bastard! Oh my God!"

As the afternoon sun coming through the window waned, we slowed down. Emily turned and threw her arms around me, dragging me down onto the bed beside her.

To my surprise, my feisty aunt took me into her arms and put her mouth on mine, and we slipped into a most beautiful kissing moment that seemed to last forever. Without looking at me, she bowed her head and snuggled up against my chest, and I thought I felt her sobbing continue. I rubbed her shoulders and nibbled at her ear. No one spoke.

The phone rang, and Emily reached out and answered.

"Yes, Sis, he's still here?"

"No, he's staying with me tonight."

Then she hung up.

I ventured to reach behind her and caress her beautiful backside, and when I lovingly groped a buttock, this remarkable woman pushed her bum at my hand. A whisper accompanied the movement.

"My kink belongs to you now, Roger. Forever!"

Emily moved her head and peered up at me. Her eyes had that mysterious look from long ago which I couldn't quite place, and she smiled lovingly. Then in her whispering voice, she made a final request.

"Don't forget the belt, Roger. But let me dream about it until the morning. Then you can give it to me so hard that I come like the slut I am.

"Then I will want you to fuck me as you did before. My punishment will be my heavenly reward."

FIVE

MY ENLISTMENT

I wasn't going to, but I just couldn't pass up the offer.

It had been a couple of weeks since my interaction with the wonderful Julie. Although I had an open invitation to meet up with her again, the vision of Mary's backside at our sex education class was still vivid in my mind. I definitely wanted to get better acquainted with it.

It was five o'clock on a Monday afternoon, and I was inside the Charity shop, and I had already told the assistant that I was looking for shirts. She smiled knowingly and said that although they were about to close, she would call someone she thought would help me.

Mary laughed when she saw me, and she took my hand, indicating a level of intimacy.

"I thought I'd lost you to my best friend Julie, Roger. She spoke very highly of you."

I felt myself blushing and felt a little foolish.

The other shop assistant called 'goodbye' and left and Mary went and locked the door. Then she came and retook my hand and led me past the clothes racks to the little restroom where I had enjoyed her friend.

In just seconds, Mary unhitched her skirt and let it drop. Then she pushed me onto the little bed and climbed on top of me and beamed down a smile of promise while she groped the growing bulge in my trousers.

"Now show me what that bitch Julie enjoyed so much. I want to try it!"

Laying back while this super sexy woman swallowed and sucked my stiff cock made me realise just how much I enjoyed sex. I might still lack experience, but Julie and my aunt Emily and now Mary were sufficient to prove to me that as far as human activity went, making love with a woman must surely be the pinnacle of a man's endeavour.

While Mary was busy, I took the opportunity to explore her magnificent rear end with my hands. Vast expanses of smooth, soft buttock welcomed my fingers, and I trembled with excitement. Then I let a finger trace the path that hid between her buttocks, discovering a small damp spot in the centre, and I shook even more.

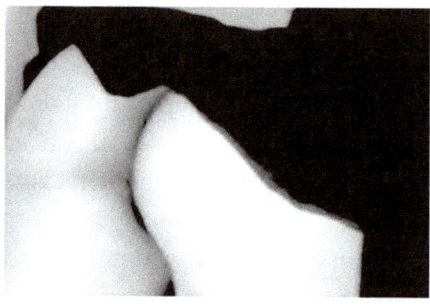

Mary stopped sucking and lifted her head and looked up at me, and spoke in a super soft voice.

"You want it don't you Roger? You want my bum, I can tell. It would please me greatly if you fucked my big arse, you beautiful young man. It's something I really enjoy but rarely find anyone volunteering for. So are you ready for a ride on an ocean liner, Roger?"

I looked into her smiling eyes and smiled back. "Oh yes, Mary! Lead the way."

Mary rolled over onto her knees.

"Reach over and get that tube of lube on the side cupboard, and while you are at it, get yourself a condom from the draw. You should always wear a condom for anal sex. Then you should get rid of it before getting back into a vagina."

I obeyed my large mistress, and with her guidance, I was suddenly staring down at that part of her anatomy I'd dreamt about constantly.

Mary reached back and pulled open her buttocks to show me the freshly lubed pink orifice in which she intended to engulf me. Then, not waiting for me to act, she reached back with a hand and guided the end of my cock to the magic door.

"Now push in hard, darling. I want it!"

I did as I was instructed, discovering the second heavenly gate a woman could offer a man.

"Oh yes, Roger, yes, yes. Push it in harder, you darling man. You won't hurt me."

I was on fire, and that manly thing that had happened with Emily happened again. I was suddenly working out and pushing this magical piece of gym equipment to its limits. Mary yelled more "yes's" and "harder", and she reached back and grasped my backside and pulled me up against her buttocks and held on tight so that I could not escape.

I joyfully rode her ocean liner through waves and troughs, and all the while, Mary moaned and sang and called out incoherently. And then I yelled, and Mary pushed her arse up to meet me while I filled it with my cum. And after a few moments of Mary fingering herself, she screamed "yes" then lay flat on the bed.

Riding Mary's ocean liner was something I will never forget. In the months and years that followed, Mary would sometimes text me or say on the phone that she would like to go to sea again, and if I could get to her, I would, and I would mount her huge soft shapely rear, and she would take us both to heaven. Sometimes I would slap a buttock, snap her suspenders against her white thighs, or drag my fingernails down her back, wanting her to know that for those few moments, she belonged to me.

Never was it anything other than a joyous, wonderful moment, and our mutual satisfaction was always assured.

One day, I received a call from Mary, who said that she and Julie would like to meet with me for coffee, cake, and a chat. I happily agreed, and we made a time. I met them at the coffee shop just along from the Charity Shop.

Two hands reached out for mine, and two sets of lips offered themselves up to me as I arrived. This was so nice, seeing two of my favourite women at one time.

I settled down and ordered Carrot cake and a long black coffee and looked from one to the other of these enchanting women.

"Well, this is a wonderful surprise. Is it a special occasion?"

The two looked at each other and then at me.

"We are here to proposition you, Roger. So please hear us out."

I was taken aback. These ladies need never propose anything we didn't already enjoy together. I felt I belonged to them, body and soul, and they could demand anything they liked from me.

"Well, then! Let's hear it. You know I'm besotted with both of you, so I'm only capable of saying yes."

The two giggled and looked at each other.

"You know, Roger, that we are both registered sex workers?"

"I do."

Mary spoke first.

"Well, our association is an excellent organisation, but it lacks one thing. Men! We don't have enough men. And before you ask, yes, plenty of men put themselves forward, but rarely do we find any of them suitable.

"Julie and I think you are very suitable. You have looks, charm, masculinity, and above all, you are intelligent. There was a fifth thing Julie? I can't remember what it was?"

Julie smiled across the table at me.

"He has a very lovely cock, Mary. How could you possibly forget?"

"Ah yes! Of course. How could I forget?"

"Well, Roger, the pay is good, we believe you would enjoy the work, and you have the backing of a very supportive group of fellow workers. The job would likely involve you in two, three or sometimes four or more liaisons a week. The association collects the money and passes it on to you at the end of the following month."

I was madly trying to process what my lovely ladies were saying, but it wasn't easy. The questions were uppermost in my mind: 'where', 'when' and 'how could I do it. Never once did I question if I should do it.

Moral and ethical questions seemed to be absent from my head. Thoughts were tumbling about.

"I don't have my own place?" I mumbled sheepishly. "But I will be getting an apartment quite soon, I expect."

I was wildly imagining or attempting to imagine what this line of activity would be like. It was obviously sexual. But would I enjoy it? And would I become a very different person? I looked closely at my two companions. They didn't seem strange or unattractive. I thought I should stall by asking questions.

"What sort of things would I be looking at doing?"

Julie answered me with a loving smile.

"Attitude is everything. You need to be of a particular positive state of mind that allows you to view situations through loving eyes.

"Giving is the best way to receive, and none could be equal to giving another human being love. That is why it's called the oldest of the four recognised professions. Yes, it might be physical, but the result is mental and emotional."

I thought about what Julie said. If I thought about it, both she and

Mary had expressed themselves towards me with extraordinary love and affection.

"Perhaps a woman can give what a man might not be able to? Could you give me an example of what I might be asked to do? That might help me."

Mary and Julie looked at each other, obviously thinking how best to answer me. Julie leant down and took a piece of paper from her bag.

"This is a list of four inquiries for a male escort that we received over the past seven days. I'll use aliases to protect people's privacy.

"Alison is a widow. She has been on her own for three years and misses male company. She and her husband were together for nearly thirty years. Alison says she wants a man for gentle play and maybe sex.

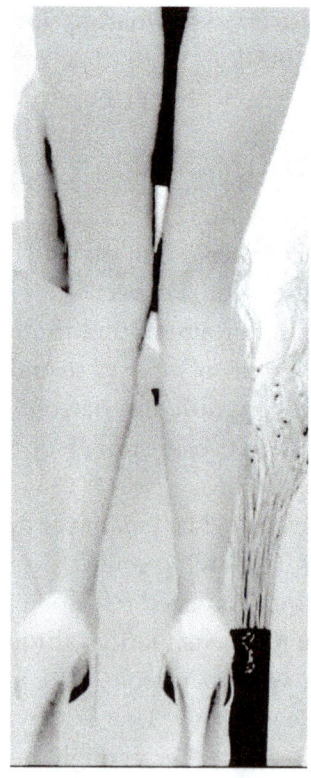

"Angie has never married. She has recently recovered from a lifetime of anorexia and is very thin. She wants a man she can touch and who will touch her despite her skinny body.

"Cherie calls herself a slut but a late starter. She wants to make up for lost time and have good sex with a man. She hopes we might be able to offer her the real thing. She's sick of weak men.

"Lastly, we have Doreen and Sharon, who live in the same house. Doreen likes to claim they need a man because Sharon has never had one, and Doreen wants to be sure her friend is safe and looked after.

"That is their story. But we happen to know more about these two, thanks to a tip-off from another agency. It turns out that they are both very experienced and both are desperate for a man, so desperate that they will happily pay the double rate and extra time if needed. We are not sure why they are not just giving it away to all comers. Still a bit of mystery about this one."

Mary laughed and thanked Julie. "There will always be a mystery client somewhere."

Then the two looked at Roger for his response.

"Oh yes, Roger, I should also have mentioned that your take-home from these would be around $1000, give or take a $100."

Mary could see that I was thinking long and hard about their offer.

"I don't want to downplay the money side of things, Roger, but the job is very much about what a strong person can offer others, and it also is about enjoying the job and having a good time. And we should mention, Roger, that you can sign up for a 30 day trial period. This will give you and our people a chance to explore whether it suits you and our team."

Mary's advice sealed it for me. I can't deny that I was excited by the idea of having sex with strangers. The idea also touched some buried aspect of my new manly growing-up feelings that were constantly telling me to go forth and conquer or was that simply libido.

"I'll try it then! But only the first three on the list. The idea of two at once doesn't appeal to me, at least not at the moment."

Big smiles welcomed my decision.

"Well, that's good news, Mary. The bad news is that he doesn't want a threesome with us. Just as I was about to suggest it, too."

"They are my thoughts, too, Julie. Maybe we can lure him somewhere one day with promises of a visit to a double heaven, and then the two of us could have our way with him."

I could feel myself blushing and, at the same time, getting hot at the thought of having my two favourite whores laying there together and displaying themselves and inviting me to feed on them.

"So, welcome aboard, Roger. We'll get you a printed copy of the contract and rules.

"For the moment, we should tell you that the association – we like to call it the club – has access to several motel rooms around Sydney, plus it owns a couple of apartments. When you have a booking, you will be told where to meet the client and given the entry key code and address where you will meet, along with the client's name and any further details.

Mary looked at me and then at Julie.

"It's now just a matter of when you want to start? We suggest you give yourself a few days grace so that you can read your contract and get yourself prepared.

"We think you will be a wonderful sex worker, Roger. I'm sure we would both want to book you! Now does our new colleague have any questions? It's a good time to ask."

There was just one odd question that intrigued me.

"What are the most common reasons that cause a man to leave the club?"

The two giggled, and each suggested the other should answer. It was Julie who spoke.

"Wealthy women constitute a significant problem. The offer of a good life in a villa on the Riviera or in Milan or Paris in return for being the woman's permanent toy-boy can be very tempting.

"The club lost two good male workers only last year. Both have since reappeared and asked for the jobs back, but it's a policy that they do not get rehired under any circumstances. The reason for this is that they could do the same thing again.

"It has happened at another agency where a worker took off to Europe three times with three different clients. It also meant the loss of those clients."

I was intrigued. This looked like a ticket to the fast lane, a backstop, if ever I wanted to move on.

"Sometimes, a man will suffer a temporary loss of libido and will ask for time off. We're always sympathetic and supportive.

"We girls are sometimes confronted with the same CGO syndrome. CGO stands for Can't Go On. But it's usually temporary and something we can manage to live with, unlike the obvious problem that a man might suffer."

I signed a contract a few days after being conscripted by my loving fellow workers. I'd even sorted a nom-de-plume. My pen name was Carlos. Now I just had to wait for my first assignment.

When it came, I was immediately intrigued. Angie, the anorexic sufferer, was to be my first customer, and I liked the idea. A gentle start to my new job appealed to me. Or so I thought.

SIX

ANOREXIC ANGIE

I arrived at the motel unit twenty minutes early, wanting to be available to welcome Angie.

It was sparse but comfortable. There were nice things to eat and drink in the fridge, and everything seemed set for my first adventure as a sex worker.

Angie was different to what I had expected. Not the sad, dour woman lacking self-confidence that somehow I'd imagined she would be.

"Hello, Carlos! Pleased to meet you. You look yummy! Are we allowed to eat? I brought sandwiches in case we got hungry. Where do you want to start? You're my first man in at least ten years. I'm actually really looking forward to it."

Angie was refreshingly straightforward, and I was temporarily lost for words.

"Hi, Angie! So pleased to meet you. And yes, we can eat as much as we like. And yes, I'm looking forward to it too."

Introductions over, we surveyed each other with smiles. I thought Angie's smile was indicative of her anticipation of what she thought she was about to experience. In my mind, I was not just rallying the troops but also wrestling with strategy.

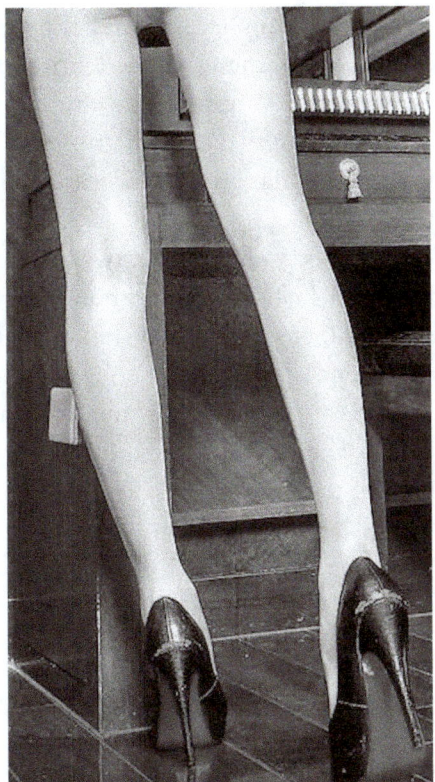

Lust was my new best friend. I looked at Angie's slender body.
Then I imagined myself lifting the hem of her short dress and placing
myself between her shapely but skinny legs. Moments later, I felt a
response to that thought in my trousers. Liftoff!

Angie sensed my interest and looked down at my trouser front. She
reached towards it and pressed her hand against me. Then she leant
her head towards mine and whispered.

"Oh, Carlos! So soon! I'm not sure that I'm quite ready. What
happens now?"

I turned Angie's head and kissed her gently.

"I'm in no hurry to do anything, sweet lady. I just want to love you
and enjoy a leisurely time together."

Angie moaned and found my lips, and we swam in a most
delightful pool of cautious passion.

I ran my hand up to her tiny chest and playfully touched her through her blouse, not knowing if such small breasts would enjoy my attention. But they did, and Angie reached up and unbuttoned her blouse and led my hand inside, presenting my fingers first with one and then with the other of two very stiff nipples. I ventured more fingers onto the surrounding flat breasts and caressed her, and the dear lady moaned in appreciation.

Angie wanted just to keep kissing me. It was like she was starved for affection, and while I knew nothing about her private life, from what she had already said, I assumed that she lived alone although she could have a woman friend.

I was enjoying her kissing starvation if that is what it was. It was so beautiful and relaxing. Then I felt her exploring my belt buckle and knew she was preparing to move on.

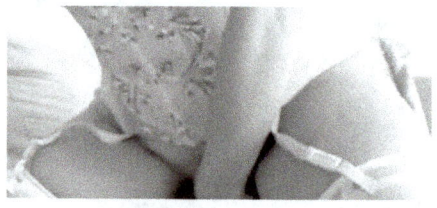

As Angie moaned and stroked and squeezed my cock, I ran my hands up under her skirt and drew down her knickers. Then I whispered that I wanted to see more of her, and she gasped.

"Be my guest, Carlos."

I backed Angie to the edge of the bed then turned her around. She immediately volunteered to bend over, and I lifted her skirt.

A perfect little bum stared back at me, and a patch of dark, moist pubic hair sat between her legs, calling for my attention. I gently touched her, and she shook all over, murmuring, "Oh yes, Carlos!"

Elegant was the word that came to mind when I looked at her and caressed her tiny buttocks.

The thinness of her legs holding up a remarkably slender body put me in mind of fairies from those magic picture books of my childhood. I imagined this delightful creature wafting around amongst the hollyhocks and floating on sunbeams on a summer afternoon, taunting pixies in the same way that she did to a mere unaware seven-year-old.

"Do you like me?"

The ever-inquisitive voice of Angie broke the spell.

"Will I do?"

Oh, how lovely she was. Her simple response to my carnal investigations made me want to love and adore her, but then I realised that this was likely to be an ever-present danger in a sex workers life.

"You are so beautiful, Angie. Are you ready for me, lovely lady? There is no need to rush if you would like more time?"

"Yes, Carlos, I'm very ready for you. And afterwards, we might have time for a sandwich and a drink followed by another cuddle? Would you like that? I hope we will have time for more?"

Angie was both a fairy and an angel. She just lacked wings. But now we were about to fly.

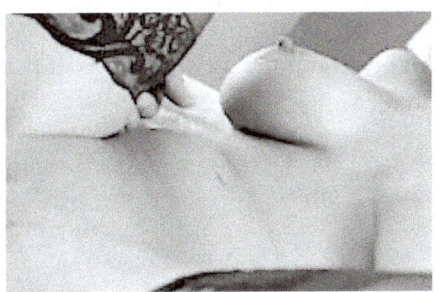

I put the head of my cock against her moist vulva, and to my surprise, delicate pink lips opened and all but sucked me in. Suddenly I was right up inside Angie, and she was ecstatically calling out my name.

"Oh, my God, Carlos, that is so beautiful!"

As I joyfully shafted this sensitive and unusual woman, I leant forward over her back and found an ear and told her that I wanted to do this forever, and then again after we'd had afternoon tea. My pronouncement excited Angie so much that she gave a little scream, and her tiny body shook so much I had to clutch her tightly around the waist to prevent my penis from being evicted.

"Oh, Carlos! You are so good. Oh, God! Lookout! I'm coming again."

I hung on as Angie threw her body around in her second huge orgasm.

"Oh my God! I never knew about any of this. You are incredible. Please don't take it out."

Angie snuggled up and sobbed a little and giggled a little and played with my now flaccid cock. Every little while, she would reach up to kiss me.

After we'd eaten her cucumber and eggs and lettuce sandwiches and drank coffee from her flask, Angie came and cuddled up to me and kissed my neck. Then she lifted her head and whispered in my ear, "If you wanted to, I'd love it if you fucked me again, Carlos."

I slid my hand behind her little bum and swung her around. Then, with her skinny legs bent and wide apart, we quietly shagged away the rest of our time together. Angie came twice again and then covered me with kisses.

"I think you will be seeing me again, Carlos, if that is okay?"

"I would love that, Angie."

SEVEN
CHERIE THE SLUT

Cherie's description of herself as a slut sounded ominous, only because I had no experience with such self-described women.

My stepmother once, in the heat of the moment, described aunt Emily as a bloody slut. But I was very young, and it meant nothing to me. A couple of years later, I looked up the word and was shocked to discover it meant a woman with many casual sexual partners and a woman who is 'sexually promiscuous.

My recent experience with Emily, who happily wore the epithet, had convinced me that a slut was always going to be someone I could work with.

So if nothing else, I knew that if Cherie was being even half truthful, she was very experienced.

I wondered why she was prepared to pay for sex when she knew her way around. Surely, she couldn't have run out of men?

The bell rang, and I opened the door. A film-star-like vision stood in the doorway, smiling seductively. She wore a full-length fur coat, leather gloves and stockings and high heels. I couldn't immediately be sure what I was looking at because of the large, heavy coat but I was sufficiently inspired by her lower legs, ankles and feet to make me feel optimistic.

"Cherie?"

"Unless you are expecting someone else, you handsome man. Do I need to get in line, or will we all be doing things together? I'm more than happy to get undressed and watch until it's my turn?"

I laughed politely at what she had said and invited her in.

"I think just the two of us would be preferable, Cherie. Even the little I've seen of you so far suggests I will happily have my hands full."

Cherie laughed, seemly appreciating my comment, and walked over to the bed. Then she turned and put her arms out towards me.

"Come here and find out what I've brought you."

As I moved towards the lipsticked bright-eyed vamp, Cherie laughed and let her fur coat fall open in front of me, exposing a pair of exquisite naked breasts, and then she slipped it off and threw it in a corner. She stood in all her womanly splendour except for her panty-hose and her stylish stilettos.

The way she held her body, turned a leg or arm or turned up her stiletto clad feet oozed sexuality. I immediately wanted to eat her; then I wanted to simply fuck her till I couldn't fuck her anymore.

Cherie cupped a shapely breast in each hand, pushing them up and shaking them at me. Then she embraced me, and we kissed, and I inhaled the smell of her perfume and makeup.

"Are you going to fuck this poor little slut, Carlos? You can do whatever you want. I will love it! My cunt, my arse, my mouth; cum wherever you want, whatever. I fucking crave it constantly. I can't get enough cock. Say you want to give it to me, you beautiful man."

Then Cherie turned and flopped onto the bed, and I looked down on her substantial legs and buttocks and hastily unpacked myself.

"You are beautiful, Cherie, and yes, I want to fuck you until you scream."

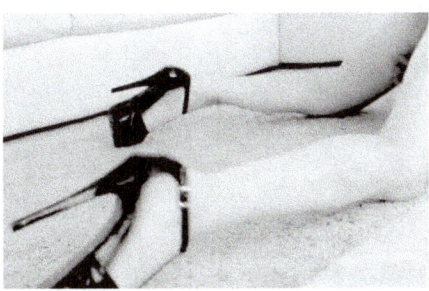

I lifted her feet and removed her shoes. Then I peeled down and pulled down her pantyhose and gazed down on her most adequately styled body. She knew exactly where I was and what I was looking at, and automatically she reached behind her and waved her hand around close to my cock, trying to take hold of me.

I pushed my cock so that it touched her hand, and suddenly I was firmly in her grasp and her prisoner.

Cherie quickly rolled over. With her spare hand, she dragged me down onto the bed beside her, then she hovered over me and fed me into her mouth, moving her head up and down and slurping and moaning. Then she removed her mouth and looked up at me.

"Your cock is beautiful. You might never get it back, young man. I'm going to suck and fuck you all night. Just put it on the bill."

We fucked on and on and in every orifice. I quickly ignited the fire that saw me loving Cherie like I loved my time in the gym working out. And when I dared to stop and ask if she would like a small pastry and a drink, Cherie mumbled back.

"Sure! Just so long as it's quick and you can still fuck me some more. You really know what to do with your equipment."

EIGHT
ALISON ALL ALONE

After my first two experiences as a sex worker, I decided I would not try to anticipate what the next client would be like. I wondered if this was my first piece of perceived wisdom resulting from just a short time on the job.

The bell rang, and I went and opened the door.

"Welcome, Alison! I'm Carlos, as you probably guessed."

I ushered in a pleasant but plain-looking older woman. She carried a little more weight than she probably wanted to, but she seemed personable and smiled politely.

"Hello, Carlos. Pleased to meet you."

I suggested she sit in the large armchair, feeling that the sofa might be too up close and personal. She had the air of one who was not very comfortable with this unfamiliar situation. I didn't want to alarm her unnecessarily.

My appointment instructions included a 'maybe' in front of the word sex. Soft play seemed to be the main request. I also had a hunch that she might feel that I was too young for her.

"We've got nice soft freshly squeezed juice, or I can offer you a Yorkshire Tea, Alison. I prefer it to English Breakfast. Not sure why;

they are very similar. And we've got some chocolate wheaten biscuits. Dark chocolate, not milk chocolate."

My conversation about things one might consider mundane worked, and Alison showed a beautiful smile and said she would love to try the tea.

I boiled the jug and popped bikkies on a plate and served them on the little table between the sofa and the armchair, complete with a jug of milk, teabag squeezers and a small bowl for the used tea bags.

After I had served the tea, I sat back and encouraged Alison to talk. As we settled down, I noticed the hem of her dress had moved up while she was reaching for a biscuit, and I caught a glimpse of a nice pair of legs and her tanned stockings held up with suspenders.

I would have expected her to wear pantyhose, so a glimpse of suspenders caused me to wonder if she had been advised that this look would work best in this situation. Along with her sensible low-heeled brogues, I appreciated her mostly conservative clothing choices.

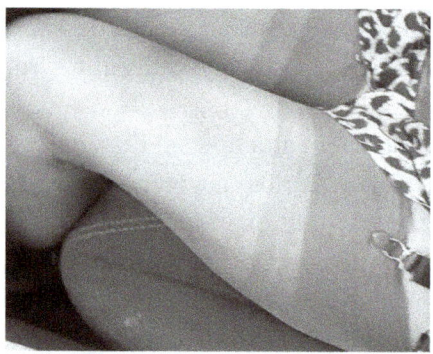

Alison told how she had married George when she was eighteen and how he was the first and only man she'd ever been with. She looked wistfully into her cup.

"It was never a very happy marriage. He never seemed to be satisfied with me. I just couldn't seem to give him what he wanted. I suppose being so young and innocent, the world's ways were alien to me, and George simply found me boring.

"But he left me a wealthy widow. Most women would be happy with that."

I listened sympathetically to Alison's story, wondering how on earth we could change the world so that these great sadnesses could be avoided.

I tuned back in when I realised she was telling me something that seemed important.

"I'm so sorry, Alison. Would you mind repeating that? I had a sudden moment of panic. I thought I'd forgotten to do something important, then realised I had in fact, done it. So sorry!"

"That's all right, Carlos. I was about to tell you that I have recently met a man I like very much and he appears to like me. I so want to be the woman he would want to be with. I thought if I spent some time with someone like you, you might teach me the things I never learnt in my younger days."

Wow! No one told me that this job came with that level of responsibility.

I looked at Alison. Her face had changed from the sad older lady who knocked on the door to an attractive bright-eyed woman who wanted the world. And looking at her in a new way brought forth new ideas.

"Well, Alison. You've really put me on the spot now. You would like me to show you sexual manoeuvres with which to bond with your new man? But I know nothing about him or come to think of it, about you?

"Do you or he want to explore sucking and licking each other? Do you want to masturbate him or encourage him to do that to you? And will he prefer you in a missionary position or a doggy pose on your knees? What turns people on is a very personal thing. Am I qualified to take on this huge responsibility?"

I looked at Alison. She was staring back at me with her mouth partly open. Then in a quiet little voice, she answered the question.

"Yes, to all of that, Carlos, and can we start with the masturbating thing, please? Show me what to do, young man. I'm your willing pupil. And Carlos, I'm feeling really excited. Or perhaps I'm feeling horny. Is that the word?"

That was the moment when I stopped overthinking things.

"We are going to make love, Alison. I'll keep it simple, and I want you to tell me if you don't want me to keep doing anything to you that you're not enjoying. You can also ask me for more of something if you need more practice or you simply just like it. Is that clear? Now you had better come over here where I can get my hands on you."

As quick as a flash, Alison was standing in front of me and in just a couple more moments, I had her dress over her head and her bra on the floor. I asked her to remove her shoes and knickers, and suddenly, the now super keen sexy well-built and fleshy lady was naked and bent over with her face down close to my trouser front, keenly watching me unbuckling myself.

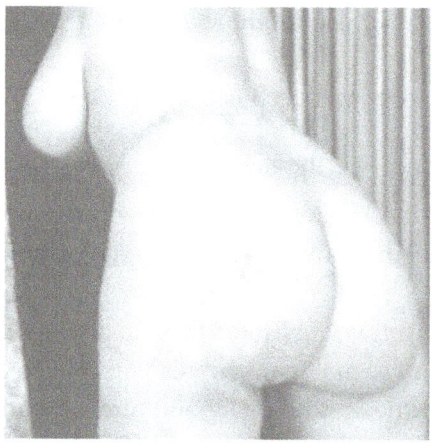

Alison moved her face down closer to view my now fully erect member as it came into view, her breasts dangling freely and jiggling on my knees.

I took her hand and wrapped her fingers around it, and said quietly, "There, Alison, congratulations. Now gently rub it up and down. Here! I'll show you how it's done."

Alison was quick to learn and tackled me like someone given a task to do in the kitchen. Her matter of fact manner caused me to reflect on what we'd done so far. Kissing! I hadn't yet kissed her. That should have come first.

I swept a hand up over the bending woman's large buttocks, excited by a woman's bum as always. "I'll be back," I told myself.

I lifted Alison's chin and smiled, and she smiled back.

"Is this okay?"

"Yes, Alison, but I do want to kiss you, dear lady. Kissing is so important."

I removed her hand from my cock and encircled her upper body with my arms, and turned her and eased her onto my lap. Then I lifted her chin and put my lips on hers.

My cock was lost between her buttocks and her hairy vulva, and I felt her trying to adjust herself so that we were both comfortable.

Alison was new to kissing. Her lips were taut, and her mouth clamped shut.

"Open your mouth just a little, please Alison, and poke your tongue out so that we can kiss like Romeo and Juliet."

It didn't take long for Alison to discover the joys of kissing.

After my initial foray with my tongue, she responded with gusto. She pushed her tongue as energetically into my mouth as she could, swishing it from side to side and slurping profusely.

I had to admit that I fully appreciated her enthusiasm. I lay back while the lovely woman explored her newly discovered ability to please, urged on perhaps by my lovingly fondling her shiny, soft derrière.

Alison stopped her kissing and moved her head so that she could look into my eyes, "Kissing is wonderful, Carlos. I just wish I'd found out forty years ago."

It was time to move along. I pushed the dear woman back and fixed her with a smile.

"We are going to make a big move now, Alison. I want you to kneel on the sofa. We are going to start with the doggy position. Now, are you okay with that?"

The poor woman looked at me as though I was about to throw her off a cliff. Without further discussion, I rose and turned her and helped her into position. Then I palmed her pussy and kissed and licked her buttocks, and waited for her response.

"Okay, so far?"

"Yes, Carlos! All good!"

Once we began to fuck, Alison was transformed. Suddenly, she was the fully sexual being that she wanted to be. We moved in unison, and she counter-thrusted when I plunged energetically into her.

When I moved her onto the carpet and rolled her onto her back, she responded, lifting her legs and spreading them wide apart and bending her knees. She even reached out for me and guided me through her wet hairy covering where I plunged in and energetically fucked her, listening as she moaned while looking at her broad contented smile.

When I thought it was time to stop, Alison sat up and pulled my cock between her lips, and we ended the day with an extended sucking session. I volunteered a reciprocal sucking on her noticeably large clitoris, and she came, pulling my face in closer.

"Oh, Carlos. That was so nice. Please do it again."

I did, and she came again. Life for Alison was good, and for me too.

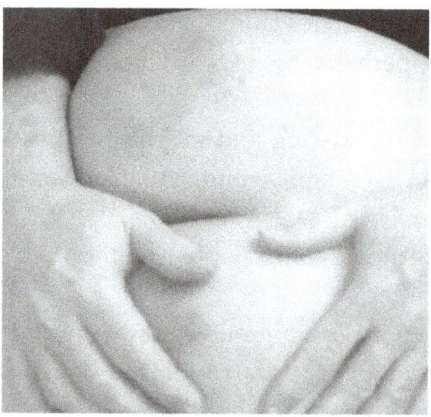

Alison giggled when I asked if I could play with her beautiful bottom before she got dressed.

"Oh, Carlos! I love it that you find me desirable. This has been the most enjoyable and life-confirming moment of my life. Can a girl book you for another visit? Can I be sure that it would be you who I came to?"

"Yes, Alison, I'll make certain of it. I'd love to see you again. But I must warn you. I can be a bit kinky, and I love your bum so much I might want to spank it or do even ruder things to it."

"Oh yes, Carlos, you darling man. We'll definitely meet again."

NINE

REFLECTING ON THE FIRST 12 WEEKS

I had been a sex worker for 12 weeks, and the more clients I saw, the more I enjoyed myself; and I liked to believe that they enjoyed their time with me.

Each was memorable in its own way. Even the most common reason for a liaison which was recently widowed wives, now missing out on sex became a worthwhile endeavour. Hopefully, each experienced their inner feeling writ large, or perhaps I should say, writ totally naked and fucked. And I felt love, however odd that might sound.

It was a feather in my cap that I was also developing a following.

Widow Alison had revisited me, and while all had gone very well, especially when she smiled lovingly at me and proffered a wicked look.

"Now, Carlos! You showed interest in my bottom when we first were together. I've been reading about what can be done with a bum. I'm quite excited about it but a bit nervous. So how about you have your way with it? I know you'll be gentle with me. Are you still interested?"

Cherry, the self-styled slut had also returned, telling me that she had yet to find someone as good as me.

"Just give me what I had before, Carlos. And don't hang back on the rough stuff."

There was the odd thing or two that occurred that I hadn't anticipated. My youngest woman ever, Chloe, a delightful woman in her late twenties, asked if I made house calls. I hadn't given this a lot of thought but remembered seeing something in my contract which mentioned it.

"I'm fairly new on the job and haven't been asked to make house calls so far. However, I understand that the Collective allows us to visit a client with a handicap or who may be incapacitated. Does that answer your question, Chloe?"

"Yes, that's great! My sister, Lottie, is in a wheelchair. Now I've been with you and had this opportunity to sort of bond, I believe she might like to meet you.

"Lottie was in a car accident when she was 19, and now she is 29. She's not had a boyfriend since the accident. Lottie is fully functional and beautiful, and she can stand up and do everything except walk."

Chloe eyed me carefully, a wise look on her face.

"From what I've seen of you, I believe you could be trusted to do the right thing by her. You seem like a gentleman?"

I told Chloe to call the office and tell them that I was okay with her request.

It's now a couple of week later, and I've just received my list of upcoming assignments. They include a Lottie from Eros Crescent in Woollahra, requesting a home visit. This promises to be a new experience.

TEN

TEAM SPIRIT

It was late in November when I had a message from the office reminding me that the Collective would be holding its annual end of year party and an opportunity to meet my fellow workers. It said that I didn't need to dress up, but the theme would be, as always, 'A Slutty Christmas'.

I replied that I looked forward to it and marked it in my calendar.

It wasn't until I was talking to Julie that I thought to ask a question.

"Julie? How many people are likely to be at the Christmas party?"

I was a little taken aback by her reply.

"Oh, of course, it's your first. I forgot. Probably close to a 150 or more, I expect. That includes family and relatives. You are allowed to bring one other person.

"My husband will be there, of course, and this year my daughter has indicated she would like to take a walk on the wild side with mum and dad. I'm a bit concerned for her, though. She's young and good looking and will definitely attract some of our more sexually predatory colleagues.

"But I'm really looking forward to it. You will come, won't you, Roger? Be careful of my daughter, though. She's looking for a strong, silent, slightly shy type of guy."

We both had a good laugh, especially when I cautiously mentioned that I was more nervous about meeting her husband.

When we'd finished talking, I couldn't help feeling that my world had just changed.

A woman who I loved and had enjoyed fucking twice and who I looked forward to being happily between her legs again was bringing her husband and daughter to her workplace and would be introducing them to me.

One thing I'd so far never had to do was meet a lover's husband. So much to think about. And what was that about members bringing one guest? How was it the Julie was bringing two?

It was a typical balmy December day for the Sex Worker's Collective end of year party. The venue was to be a large private home in the wealthy Sydney suburb of Vaucluse. I was told that the owner was a woman named Ursula, who was active in the East Sydney Swingers Club and that she was a friend of some of the SWC's management team. I discovered later that Ursula held large parties at her house for her swinger friends.

The event officially began at 3 pm and would run until midnight, offering members the possibility of a range of timing options. Some might choose to go early, while others might like a later start.

I chose the late afternoon option and strolled through the beautiful gardens and into the impressive entry and signed in.

The crowd was already quite large, and I was excited about meeting other workers.

We had been issued with yellow name tags to identify workers easily, and I pinned 'Carlos' to my shirt as I arrived.

I understood that females outnumbered males by around twenty to one in the organisation, which was understandable given that men who wanted to meet up with women made up the major part of the client base.

Whilst I was certainly interested in meeting the women, I had a strange desire to know more about the men, given that their experiences and mine must be similar. Not that I expected them to enter into detailed conversations about their work. Just eyeballing them and noting their demeanour would be interesting.

I wandered slowly into the vast lounge room where several sofas and large comfortable looking armchairs were interspersed with bench seats and small side tables.

Double doors opened onto a dining room at the far end, and I could see dining tables and chairs. The tables were set with cutlery and glasses, and people stood before a buffet, loading their plates.

On another side of the lounge, wide stairs led up to what I presumed to be bedrooms. A passageway below the stairs led to who knows where? It was indeed a very big house.

I scanned the crowd in search of familiar faces, not that I expected to see many people that I knew, but to no avail. But there was much to observe. Dressing up was obviously something that the women had looked forward to, and generally speaking, the 'Slut Christmas' theme had appealed to most of them.

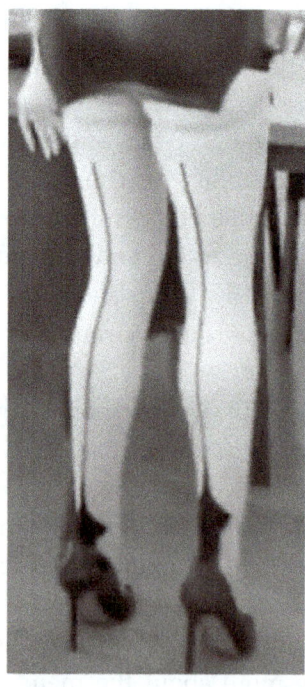

I had earlier in life come to understand that the fair sex dressed more for each other than for us mere men. And so it was at the party. A couple of punk girls with multi-coloured spiky hair, false tattoos, and amazing costumes attracted much attention when they wandered around, acting very butch and touching more girly-looking women with suggestive movements.

Mostly though, fashionable sexualised apparel graced the women and not just those wearing yellow badges.

It was then that I became aware that the majority of women had a female friend in tow. And it wasn't just the younger yellow badged ladies. Later, I discovered that many female sex workers have female partners, often, though not always, much older women. At first, this had been a shock to me, but as I gradually came to understand the female bisexual option, it just seemed to make sense. Yes, there was much to think about for a young man finding his way in life.

As the afternoon morphed into the evening, the tone changed. More daring, sexually clothed women arrived and filtered through the crowd, each attracting the eyes of the by now, slightly inebriated throng.

I was attracted, in particular, to a young woman dressed as a fairy, complete with wings, a magic wand and pointy ears. Perhaps her high heels wouldn't have appeared in Cicely Barkers Flower Fairies of The Trees, but her eyes, peering through her pretty woodland fairy mask, sparkled, and I was smitten.

Later, as I surveyed the crowd, I saw my fairy queen backed against a wall, seemingly being propositioned by a lady with lustful intent. The woman wore a simple black dress with what I could only describe as an Amazonian neckline that, on one side, dipped and exposed a very shapely naked breast.

As I watched the attempted seduction play out, two things occurred. Even as the fairy politely tried to resist having her head drawn towards the bare breast, the Amazon woman had a hand moving beneath the fairy's tiny skirt.

Then an elegant older woman walked up behind the woman whose breast was exposed, slid her arms around her waist, and groped the said object of interest. The breasted lady turned and was taken by the hand and was led away, albeit unsteady on her stilettoed feet.

The second thing that happened was that my coworker and love interest, Julie, appeared from nowhere, approached the woodland fairy, took her by the hand, and led her away through the crowd towards the opposite wall.

I was excited by at last seeing someone I knew and also by noting that Julie knew the fairy lady, and I immediately thought that this could well be her daughter.

As time went on, it seemed that as well as the extraordinary costumes in evidence, some ladies were intent on unbuttoning or unzipping themselves or others, even removing some of their outer clothing and displaying themselves in their underwear. And this was much appreciated by the rest of the crowd.

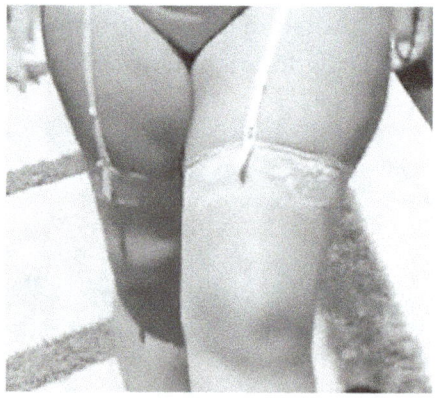

It occurred to me then that given the profession that many were engaged in, having fun with their apparel and bodies on their terms, separate from their working commitments, was probably very liberating. No fumbling customers to please; only themselves and anyone who they found attractive.

I was happy just observing the crowd. I was impressed with the ladies looks, both young and old, even though I was well aware that cosmetics, along with their clothes, contributed much to their overall appearance.

For a young man, seeing so many women so extravagantly turned out was super exciting, and the movement constantly reminded me of what hung between my legs that this might be the most extensive smorgasbord of sensual female flesh I would ever be privileged to see all at the one time.

I thought I would go in search of Julie, but then it occurred to me that she had family with her, and for the moment, I should simply explore my surroundings.

I walked up the staircase beside me and wandered along a wide passageway.

There were doors to bedrooms on either side, and I thought I heard sounds coming from a couple of them. The last room had a bright pink door, and I opened it.

Three rooms had been made into one, and the whole place was painted pink, including the ceiling.

Framed prints depicting erotic drawings from European artists of the 17th and 18th centuries graced the walls.

There were also mattresses and pillows and bolsters scattered on the floor, and on a side cupboard stood a large bowl of flowers accompanied by a dozen squeegee bottles. A quick look showed that they were all the same and contained a water-based lubricant.

I opened a drawer and discovered a range of sex toys. A second draw contained handcuffs and leather restraining belts, small flagellation tools and things I couldn't identify. This room was made for only one thing and knowing that our host was an active member of the swinging community made everything clear to me.

In the darkened corridor downstairs, much more was happening.

On a divan hidden in the shadow of the stairs, two women had surrendered to their lust quite early in the day and were sensitively kissing and groping each other oblivious to what was happening around them.

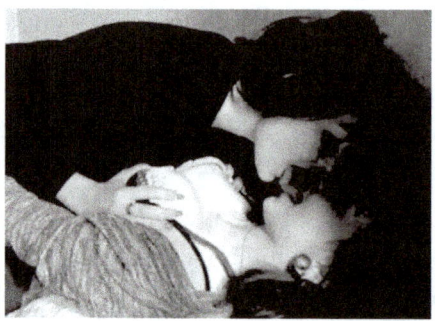

Further along and in the doorway of a darkened bedroom, a pleading voice called out gently.

"Want a girl love? Over here."

I stepped closer, and a hand took mine and placed it on a welcoming breast. I surrendered and moved closer, and suddenly I was kissing a woman I'd never met before, and not only that, my other hand was groping a second breast.

I felt a hand on my trouser front.

"Let me in, darling. I want your cock."

I quickly liberated my member, and the woman took hold of it and backed herself up against the bedroom wall beside the doorway, dragging me with her.

I didn't wait to take off her clothes. She lifted her dress and pushed the naked lower part of her body at me.

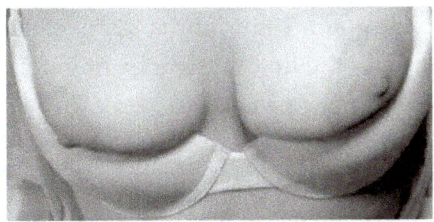

"There it is. Fuck it, you lucky man. And don't stop."

With my senses already full of images of sensual woman and their bodies, and no matter who the groaning woman might be, she was now the recipient of my unbridled lust, and she was obviously in a state of passion as well.

I hadn't, until now, known nor appreciated how great it felt to take a woman against a wall like this. It just seemed perfectly natural. Perhaps it was what happened in the past. Up against a tree, maybe. A primal coupling?

I took my time, gyrating up against the willing, sexually hungry creature as she groaned and gasped and urged me on.

"More! Yes, that's it!"

Then the woman cried out her next instruction, and I obeyed.

"On the floor, now!"

No sooner were we on the carpet, my lady captor rolled me over and mounted me and rode me, deliberately and with purpose like she was starving and had just been offered food.

After a short time, the woman screamed and arched her back and collapsed on top of me, searching for my mouth. We kissed ecstatically and groped each other in a way that only enthusiastic consenting adults can do.

As we lay still, a quiet voice asked me if I was a member or a visitor.

"I'm a member. And you?"

"Me, too. Christ, that was good. Would you like to catch up again one day? I'm Cassandra, by the way. We could fuck for fun instead of for work. What do you think?"

We still hadn't seen each other properly because of the darkened room. I knew she felt good. I ran my hands over her backside, and it felt beautiful. Then I put the tip of my index finger into her anus.

"Would you be up for play here, dear lady?"

"Sure would. I'll play there as much as you want. I'm an officially diagnosed sex addict."

"Okay, Cassandra. We'll get in touch through the club."

We enjoyed a lingering farewell kiss, and she gently massaged me between my legs.

"You said you were a sex addict. How does that work out for you, Cassandra?"

The woman sat up and looked at me through the shadows.

"I was a fat kid, and my childhood was not good. Affection came from the wrong places, and by age 19, I was picking up men for human contact through sex. Sometimes they gave me money. It wasn't long before I was on the game, a streetwalker, hanging out in doorways. Emotionally, it did it for me. But it had its dangers.

"One day, I was in the emergency waiting room at the hospital. Some bastard had got nasty. There I met a woman from the SWC, and the rest is history.

"Things are really good now. The Collective saved my life, I suppose.

"The only trouble I can get into now is of my own making. If I have a couple of drinks – as I have today – I immediately want to be back in a doorway or a laneway without my knickers on, calling out for it and hoisting my skirt and offering my cunt and getting it rough, up against a wall; but only after a few drinks. Otherwise, I get all I need through my bookings."

I stared into the darkness.

"Could you get the same feelings without having a drink, Cassandra?"

The woman peered through the shadows and hesitated before replying.

"I guess if I knew I was going to get what we just had, maybe it is possible. Are you offering?"

"Maybe in the future."

For some reason, what we'd just done had left me still feeling very horny. I found her hand and squeezed it. Then I lifted it and touched her breasts.

"I'd love you up against the wall again right now if you can manage it. Would you give me your beautiful cunt again, Cassandra?"

"Oh, God yes! Of course I will."

Cassandra jumped up and dragged me back to the wall, this time putting her hands against it, pulling up her dress over her shoulders and thrusting her backside at me.

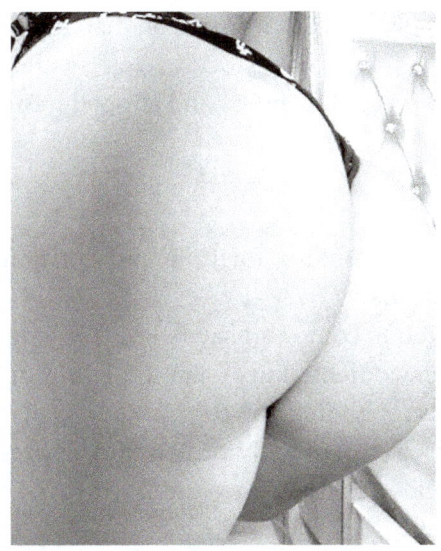

"Give it to me this way. You're a sex addict's dream come true, Carlos."

I shafted the happy lady from the rear really hard with my stiff happy cock. It felt wonderful.

"Cum in me, Carlos."

I had a massive orgasm and slumped on Cassandra's back. She turned and gently lowered me to the floor and covered me with kisses.

"Don't forget me, Carlos!"

"I won't, Cassandra."

I found a bathroom and washed and cleaned up. Then I wandered back towards the lounge room.

Music was playing, and couples and singles were dancing.

More women were now showing more of their bodies, and I imagined that maybe this was like it would be at one of the swingers parties. But then I thought about it and realised that there would be many more males hunting down the willing swinging ladies than at this event.

I looked around, searching for the men, but it was hard not to get distracted by all the female erotic forms on display.

Luscious bare thighs above stocking tops were now everywhere, and fingers played with suspenders and slipped into knickers.

I was just considering looking for Julie and her family when an arm linked with one of mine.

"Mum wants you to come and say hello. This way, please, Carlos."

The delicious woodland fairy stared up through her mask and began to lead me through the crowd.

"My mother speaks glowingly of you and assures me that you are not a bad person. She said, you are a lot like my dad. Not sure if that is a good thing or not."

As we moved slowly through the crowd, almost every woman seemed bent on showing herself to every other woman.

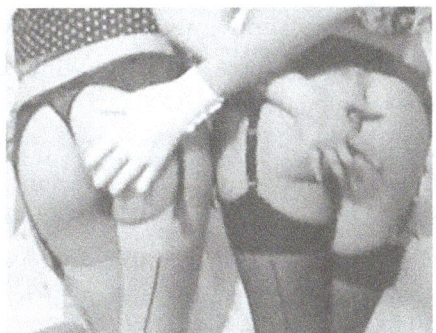

Two partly dressed women immediately in front of us were enjoying each others company, stroking each other's backsides, and it was impossible not to admire them.

The fairy lady slowed and stared, then looked up at me.

"I bet you like that?"

"It's very nice. By the way, what do I call you?"

My fairy looked up through her mask.

"Lulu will do. Everyone calls me that."

Julie welcomed me with open arms and kissed me on the mouth.

"Roger, you've met Lulu. Now please meet my husband, Brian. I've told him all about you. He said he'd already heard about you and hoped you wouldn't be stealing any of his customers."

I looked at Brian and, to my amazement, saw he was wearing a yellow label too. On it was printed, Dan.

He shook my hand enthusiastically.

"Nice to have some male company, Roger."

I was conscious of the two other members of the family watching us closely.

"Same here, Brian. You are the first male member I've met. So I'm not the only man following this lonely path?"

Everyone laughed, and then Lulu added, "I wouldn't describe it as lonely, Roger. Do you really get lonely?"

I took a punt on the wild side and answered.

"Only when I'm working, Lulu."

Brian reached out and took hold of my elbow.

"Sorry, ladies! Secret men's business!"

He moved us out of earshot then whispered in my ear.

"Firstly, Roger, try not to show any response to what I'm about to tell you. The girls will try and have some fun with you, or rather Lulu will, and her mother is on board.

"Lulu knows you, and you know her, but you haven't yet twigged who she is. She finds you interesting and will try to tease you. You do know her, her name is Lucy, and she's doing science. She likes you but complains to her mother that you never seem to notice her or ask her out. She's pretty pissed off with you. That's it mate. Best of luck."

I was shocked and immediately wanted to turn and look at my woodland fairy again, but Brian's warning stopped me. I murmured a "thank you for that, Brian."

"Okay, dad. Give him back. Stop boring him with work tips. I'm sure he manages quite well."

I moved back, and we all smiled happily.

More and more semi-clothed women were now pressing up against each other and laughingly planting kisses on bare skin on all parts of the body.

I was again fascinated by the number of younger women seemingly posturing in front of sexy looking older women. And it was no longer just fellow Collective workers.

Friends of workers who had come simply as guests and who were not wearing the yellow name tags had succumbed to overtly displaying themselves to the world. Over the heads of my companions, I could see more hand-holding women heading up the stairs, many in three's or larger groups. I figured that talk of the Pink Room had filtered through and it was about to receive a load of very happy visitors.

"So, Roger? Will you eventually meet your true love as a result of your job. Mum and dad did."

"That is not true, darling. We knew each other well before we joined the SWC, didn't we, Brian?"

"At least a week, my precious."

The family banter was wonderful, and seeing how Julie and Brian put their arms around each other's waists was delightful, and it triggered something new in me.

"Well, Lulu. I have to confess that I'm already spoken for, so you don't need to interrogate me further."

There was a stunned silence. Julie looked at me with a stare of unbelieving shock.

Lulu's face was not visible, but I heard a sudden intake of breath, and she turned and looked at her mother as though looking for advice or emotional support. Brian smiled knowingly and with a look of approval.

After a good moment of quiet, I proceeded with my plan.

"Well, that's not quite true. The thing is, the person I'm in love with doesn't know that I'm in love with her. Every time I see her she's either with a friend or she speaks first and I loose my train of thought and my nerve."

Again, there was a profound silence.

"I know how you feel, Roger. I followed Julie home for months until she reported me and I was warned off. It was only when she decided to give me a piece of her mind, that she realised I was the one."

"Well, I think that is an exaggeration, Roger. I ..."

Her daughter interrupted her.

"Mum, that is so beautiful. How come you've never mentioned it before?"

Then the fairy stood up straight and turned and addressed me defiantly.

"I think you're a weak bastard, Roger. I'm pissed off with you.

"What is it with guys that they can't show their feelings? Tell me the poor girls name and I'll bloody tell her. At least she'll get the chance to tell you what she thinks. Then maybe you can get on with your life."

I was being addressed by a very angry fairy.

"I don't think you would know her, Lulu. She's doing science at university where I'm doing law. I see her around quite a lot but she's always got lots of friends with her. And a lot of men are besotted with her, not just me."

Then came a moment I will remember for ever. Julie moved to put her arm around Brian and put her hand to her mouth. Brian stood stony faced, no doubt waiting for the *coup de grâce* and my woodland fairy stood stock still.

"Okay, okay! Her name is Lucy. There! I've never told anyone before. Happy now, Lulu?"

All the gasping and giggling and cooing noises surrounding us disappeared from my senses as the tense silence of that moment took hold.

Lulu stepped forward, ripping off her mask and throwing herself at me, pounding my chest with her fists, and yelling expletives. Then suddenly we were hugging and kissing and Lucy was crying and laughing at the same time.

"Why did you take so long, Roger. Couldn't you see I was in love with you? Oh God! You are so bloody stupid."

Julie was madly dabbing her eyes with her handkerchief and even Brian's eyes looked a little blurry.

Then Lucy took my hand, smiled at her mum and dad and led me away to find a quiet spot. My life had moved on and new emotional insights were about to envelope me and I welcomed them.

It was getting late and Lucy and I had cried and kissed and grumbled and laughed till we knew we would have to stop.

There was nothing we wanted more than simply to be with each other and although we were passionate, we were in no hurry to make out. We instinctively knew that we had plenty of time for that.

We returned and found Julie and Brian. Things suddenly became formal as Brian shook my hand and kissed his daughter and Julie kissed me, not on the lips but on the cheek, and she too, shook my hand.

Lucy and I kissed and hugged and said our farewells and I left the family to return home for a rest and to prepare for a job interview in the morning.

My mind and emotions were full of what had happened and I endeavoured to not look too closely at what was going on around me. That was not easy, especially as I passed along the darkened downstairs passageway on my way to the back door leading to the garden and the front gate. It was a haven for the large numbers of sexually hungry who now wanted what they couldn't have in public earlier, even in this free environment.

Voices called out all around, and female bodies could not be ignored. Even though I was now in love, I decided that I should not deny the wonders of sexuality but nor did I need to partake of all that was on offer. I opted to be a voyeur instead and permitted myself to stare at whatever appeared in front of me. And there was indeed, much in front of me.

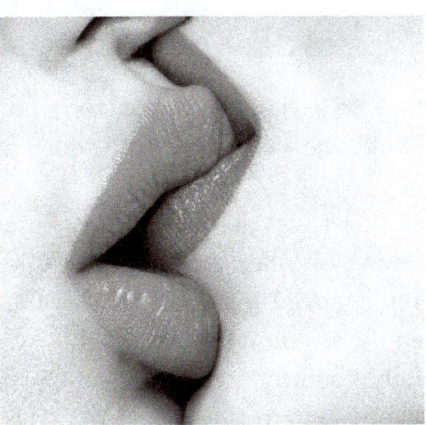

Screams of excitement and probably an orgasm sounded, and when it did, a voice from farther along the passageway happily replied with a "Yes, darling. Me, too."

There was a profound sensibility to all of these women enjoying each other, and my trouser organ told me that what I was witnessing was being appreciated.

Sometimes I dawdled and visually soaked up the passionate endeavours of the ladies around me. Once, a couple invited me to join them.

"Bring it over here, darling. We'll take it wherever you want to put it."

That was a hard one to pass up. But I managed to. I probably should have moved on more quickly, but I was enjoying things too much.

Older women were enjoying the sensitivities of some of the younger ones - sometimes with more than one - feeling every part of them and eating them out with passionate utterances.

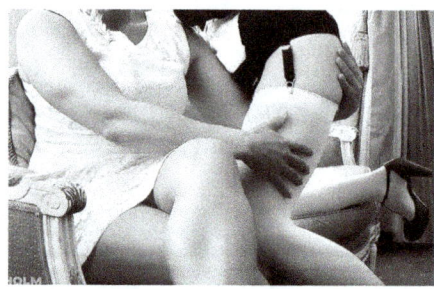

Female body parts to excite any person were on show everywhere one looked, from both the young and the more mature and I gave thanks.

It was fortunate that I was able to get out without getting myself entangled in something on offer. It was partly to do with the immediate situation of my changed relationship with Lucy and of course, I had already enjoyed the sex hungry Cassandra.

Life was definitely good for a man not yet 25 years old. I couldn't see how it could get any better.

But later, as I moved further into my twenties, my wonderful Lucy, at dinner one evening, confronted me in front of her parents, announcing that she had decided to join the Collective.

She claimed that it wasn't that she wanted to have more men in her life, she simply wanted to somehow be closer to me and share in my work. She explained that when the Collective had a female inquiry which expressed an interest in bisexual activities as well as hetero-sexual desires, we could team up and offer a double option and simply enjoy loving and giving to others, together.

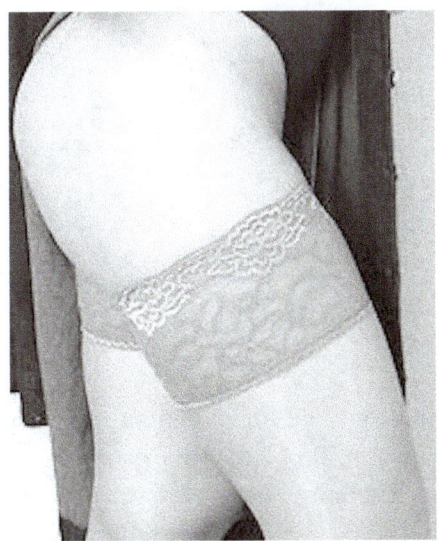

And it worked. More often than I initially expected, female clients ticked Lucy's newly added box on their application form, indicating an interest in exploring their bisexuality.

As time went on, Lucy and I expanded our services to include house calls and I lovingly introduced her to my now regular clients, Lottie and her sister Chloe. They fell in love with Lucy and she with them. We eventually became close friends and no longer bothered with commercial bookings.

This friendship and sexual arrangement lasted many years.

After a family dinner one night, Lucy announced that, having received my loving approval, she was about to make changes to her sex worker schedule.

"Well, darling. What will be different?"

Lucy had been working in a hospital as a medical consultant for a couple of years, specialising in male sexuality. She had decided that the health of many older men could benefit from an interaction with a sex worker.

"Well, mum, and you too, dad? I'm going to make myself available to older men.

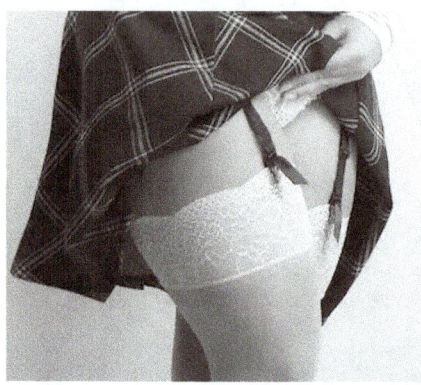

"Initially this will only be for patients from hospitals but I'll look closely at what comes in. Problems in a marriage might get added to the list, but with reservations.

"If there is going to be a problem, it will be how to remain anonymous given that I might have seen someone at my day job. Fortunately, I will see their name and can pass them on to someone else.

"It will work itself out, I'm sure. But advice from my loving family will always be appreciated."

Loving Lucy took on a new meaning every day. And when she eventually fell pregnant? Well, thats another story.

FINI

EPILOGUE

Roger and Lucy enjoyed their life together and worked out a way of living and loving which accommodated both Roger's part-time work and later, when Lucy joined the Collective, her part-time work also.

Lucy enjoyed her work as a medical scientist and the couple went on to have a family and enjoy an interesting life together.

Roger worked as a lawyer, specialising in intellectual property and copyright.

Lucy had the benefit of growing up with a loving mother and father who were both sex workers. This probably contributed to her joining the Collective and sometimes accompanying Roger to explore intimate moments with a client who expressed an interest in bisexual intimacy as well as their heterosexual proclivities.

Lucy took occasional bookings for men with sexual problems. She found that as a sex worker she could do more for men with a prostate disorder than she could through a medical solution.

Lucy would lovingly remind Roger over breakfast when they were discussing their life and their work together, "Love and romance every which way, darling. You surely couldn't get better than that."

EROS CRESCENT IN LOCKDOWN

EROS CRESCENT

These vignette's relate to characters from our well-known erotic trilogy. They were written following the Covid 19 lockdown. You will find a reference to the titles on our Richard Lee Publishing pages.

No one on Eros Crescent remembers exactly the moment when the words COVID-19 or Corona virus were first uttered in their houses. Needless to say, it would first have been heard on a television report and the importance of the message would have taken a few days to sink in.

The world suddenly changed. Words and phrases like lockdown and self-isolation and social distancing were suddenly in the forefront of all conversations as people enacted the requests of government and the nation to act responsibly to assist in the national objective to achieve what quickly became known as flattening the curve.

For Roger, life couldn't have been less affected. His daily routines required only that he rose from his bed, showered and shaved, ate his breakfast, went for a walk, and made sure he had sufficient pens and paper. Although it did impinge on his new paying project.

He had been asked by Desley to write another booklet similar to the one he'd written for The Club, only this was to be for The Dunking, a venue he had not yet visited or, until now, even heard of.

When Desley explained the concept and related what the setting inside the warehouse was like, Roger was very keen to get started. But the arrival of the virus put an end to that project, at least until further notice.

For Caroline and Jackie and Miranda, staying at home was what they enjoyed anyway, that is when they weren't travelling abroad or window shopping or having coffee in cafe's.

All three women managed to get back to Australia before the big lockdown. Each had worked in executive positions in London, but moving overseas brought that era to a close, although they had been invited to join similar companies in Australia.

A top of the range coffee making machine was promptly ordered along with a supply of fair trade East Timorese Maubisse, medium blend. Browsing online shops became the new window shopping.

Instagram took on a new importance as the pandemic took hold around the world. Stories and pictures of people in isolation doing amazing and sometime ridiculous things became the rage. Jackie uploaded hundreds of images of the inside and outside of the house, earning the praise of interior designers and architects.

Helen and her husband Frederico were effected in so far as Freddy's job as a flight controller at the airport was soon to be reduced in the number of hours he worked. However, there was no threat to his income as he was on standby as an essential service. But Helen's work as a freelance Human Resources consultant to industry came to a sudden halt. She embraced online conferencing on Zoom but this was no substitute for real hands-on consulting.

Helen was also restricted in her love life, already reduced as a result of her husbands responsibilities to her two lovers who had inadvertently become pregnant to him.

Sophie and Freya now spent a night a fortnight with Freddy.

Unable to visit or have visits from her own lovers, Polly or Celia Ashbee, Helen would just have to manage with her next-door neighbour, Mary. And what had looked like the answer to a maiden's prayer – The Club – was now the victim of a Covid close-down.

Mary's only loss of employment was her volunteer job at the Salvation Army Opportunity Shop which she would miss very much. She would also miss her sensual workout with her close friend Janice. But most of all, she would miss her newly found excitement at The Club which she had only recently discovered.

Her niece and housemate, Sophie, worked at a horse stud and accepted reduced hours and looked forward to doing baby things at home. Because she and Mary lived next door to Helen and Freddy, the two households would have access to each other when needed. And of course, Freddy was to be the father of Sophie's as yet unborn child.

Alice and Frey both lamented the loss of work in their jobs as school counsellors. They both loved their jobs. Both were pregnant and accepted they would be forced to spend more time at home together.

Like most of the others, they had their favourite sex toys for when they weren't knitting baby clothes or doing jigsaw puzzles. And like so many women in lockdown, they visited female friendly porn sites online. The two decided that they would always share these internet session and happily parked themselves on the sofa, transmitting the websites from their phones to the giant television set via a magic little box. This meant that the images were so big that they felt they were in the same room and this proved most enjoyable on many occasions.

Bertie and Rosa were the older folk who were most vulnerable to the virus. They were happy to be isolated although Bertie complained that he would miss his fortnightly get together for coffee and cake with Freddy and Roger.

Bertie complained that he still had much to say on the subject of breaking down the worlds dependance on the "couples model" as he called it.

"Nothing good will happen while we maintain this ridiculous habit of pairing off for life. Firstly, in over half the cases, it doesn't work and people separated or divorced.

"Secondly, it was obvious that people who stayed in these relationships were deeply frustrated by the repressive demands on them of constantly answering to another person.

"Thirdly, paternity and property ownership where the only reasons this system was maintained and with the likely end of democracy as we know it looming, house prices and pension funds and equity investments were likely to collapse.

"And I haven't even mentioned the problems of religion and religious wars."

Rosa looked at him. She loved him dearly but managed always to call him out.

"You haven't mentioned love once."

"Sex and love are two seperate things, my dear. We both know that."

Most of the close friends and relatives knew that Rosa and Bertie had broken up many years ago and taken lovers. Rosa entered relationships with her close girl friends and occasionally, a man.

Sometime later, she and Bertie got back together as a couple, but both maintained their freedom to embark on other relationships if they so chose, and this arrangement worked very well. It wasn't that they were desperate to take on other romantic adventures, but just knowing that they were free to do so, made the difference. They broke up after almost twenty years and had now been together for nearly fifty years.

"It was a necessary pause," agreed the two of them, lovingly.

It was Desley who had the most to lose but she wasn't particularly put out. The Club had to close only two short months after opening and only a few weeks after Desley had formed a partnership with her friend Sally who had opened The Dunking venue. The Dunking was closed too.

Desley welcomed the opportunity to take a rest and review everything about the club and the new venture and be ready to make any necessary changes or recommendations to Sally when they eventually reopened.

She and her partner Alvie, lived on the premises. Alvie knew about Desley's dalliances with Roger who she said she also had a soft spot for.

Desley had laughed, saying that now that they had so much time on their hands, she would endeavour to entice Roger to pop in for a threesome if Alvie didn't mind sharing. To which Alvie replied that she wanted first go.

Maria and her daughter Serina were at first, forced to stay home with grandfather Aldo and the boarder, Giorgio. They mostly worked for older people as cooks and housekeepers in the stately home of Vaucluse and Woollahra.

They successfully applied for positions with the council as carers so that they could continue working.

They both had each other and the two live-in men to play with when they felt like it plus a range of toys they enjoyed.

Maud, the owner of the music school and owner of the property at nineteen Eros Crescent found isolation difficult, severely limiting her adventures although she had managed to entertain herself with young Ashton and Damian after the two became suddenly sexually aware after falling prey to pizza nights with Edith.

And Sylvia and Stella, the two twenty-something country girl who she had enjoyed briefly when they stayed over on the night of her house warming party, seducing Maude with the help of their bunny party outfits, had booked in for music classes and accomodation just weeks before lockdown. Maud reasoned that a restricted lifestyle might not be too bad after all.

Life on Eros Crescent went on. The residents continued to love each other in many different ways and despite the sudden disruption of the pandemic, there was a feeling of optimism in the air.

Babies were on the way and new life called out for new ideas. And new ideas about how society worked were desperately needed.

Cross your sanitised fingers everyone, and hope.

ABOUT THE AUTHOR

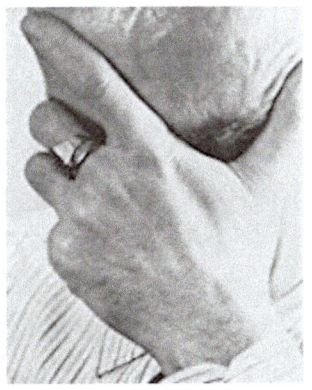

Imagine a retired writer, living in a bush hut in a forest beside a river in rural Australia. He gets lonely sometimes. Drawing on the memories of long gone days in a big city, he sets out to write simple fantasies populated with events and people he remembers.

ALSO BY RICHARD LEE

Erotic Fiction

The Eros Crescent trilogy as paperbacks or ebooks:

The Fifi Code

ISBN - 978-0-909431-02-0

Eros Crescent

ISBN - 978-0-909431-05-1

Mount Eros

ISBN - 978-0-909431-08-2

Excerpts from the Eros Crescent series as paperbacks or ebooks:

Janice: A sexual enigma

ISBN - 978-0-909431-10-5

Jessica: A young woman's journey

ISBN - 978-0-909431-13-6

Helen: Enough is not enough

ISBN - 978-0-909431-14-3

Maria: Always available

ISBN - 978-0-909431-15-0

Mary: Catching up

ISBN - 978-0-909431-11-2

The Club: Ladies love it!

ISBN - 978-0-909431-11-2

Happy Honeypots: Swinging in Harmony

ISBN - 978-0-909431-20-4

Roger: Ladies love to pay him

ISBN - 978-0-909431-21-1

Literary Fiction

Australian Short Stories

ISBN - 978-0-909431-00-6

Restless: A novel about two young men growing up
in Australia between 1900 and 1936 (Publication date not set.)

Memoir

The Kite Makers: Six years of a child's war - Britain 1939-1945

Anita Sinclair.

ISBN - 978-0-909431-16-7

Reference

Ducks for Starters: A Practical Guide to

Backyard Duck Keeping by Bruce Wicking

ISBN - 978-0-909431-18-1

Compendium Catalogue 1974: Evolution or Revolution - A facsimile. Greg
Ah Ket

ISBN - 9798743502462

Out of Print Titles

Mathematics for Young Children by Helen Western

ISBN - 978-0-909431-01-3

Currajong: For Those Whom Schools Have Failed

by Bruce Wicking

ISBN - 978-0-909431-03-7

The Puppetry Handbook by Anita Sinclair

ISBN - 978-0-909431-04-4

Wordswork by Chris Davidson & Bruce Wicking

ISBN - 978-0-909431-06-8

Sheep Production by Murray Elliott

ISBN - 978-0-909431-07-5

Sweethearts by Colin Talbot - *ISBN - 978-1-875207-02-2*

CONTACT

Publisher or review enquiries should include your full name and details in all correspondence.

Email:
lilithlovesme@gmail.com